Knights of the Endless Day

Robert Priest

VIKING

VIKING
Published by the Penguin Group
Penguin Books Canada Ltd, 10 Alcorn Avenue, Toronto, Ontario,
Canada M4V 3B2
Penguin Books Ltd, 27 Wrights Lane, London W8 5TZ, England
Viking Penguin, a division of Penguin Books USA Inc.,
375 Hudson Street, New York, New York 10014, USA
Penguin Books Australia Ltd, Ringwood, Victoria, Australia
Penguin Books (NZ) Ltd, 182-190 Wairau Road,
Auckland 10, New Zealand

Penguin Books Ltd, Registered Offices:
Harmondsworth, Middlesex, England

First published 1993

1 3 5 7 9 10 8 6 4 2

Canadian Cataloguing in Publication Data

Priest, Robert, 1951–
Knights of the endless day

ISBN 0-670-84862-X

I. Title.

PS8581.R47K55 1993   jC813'.54   C93-093412-1
PZ7.P75Kn 1993

To Daniel, Eli, Ananda and Marsha

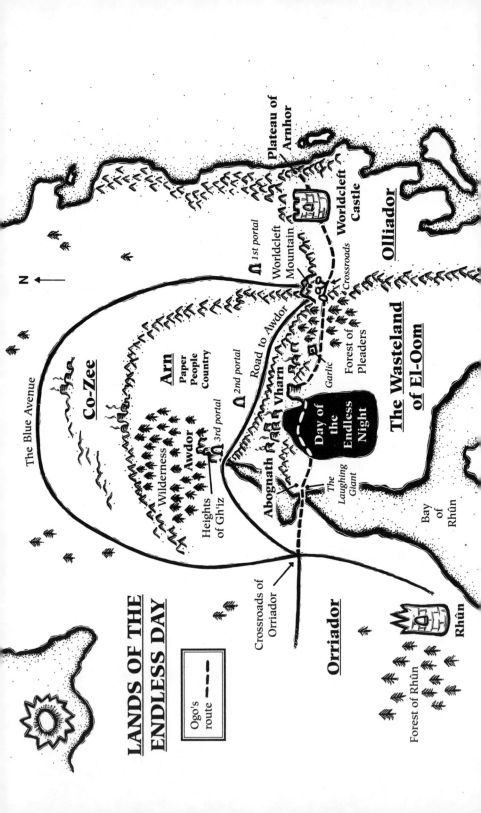

Contents

Knights
of the
Endless
Day

1

Blue Moon

In the shadows under eaves in the shadows under leaves, even in the shadow of a lone wolf who watched and waited, Moxies watched and waited. Big Moxies and little Moxies, Moxies of the mountain and tiny Moxies from the valley below. Night Moxies all, watching and listening and swaying in the shadows to the rhythm of distant hammer blows. Farther on up the mountain they could see the gigantic shadow of a figure at a forge who raised a hammer high and smashed it down hard on the anvil stone so that sparks flew.

"Hammer, hammer," he sang, all lit up in the glow of the forge and the setting sun.

> Hammer, hammer,
> Steel and coal —
> Shape this steel

1

And the steel in my soul,
This steel in the soul,
This strength of man,
The song of the iron
And the iron in my hand.

The Moxies chuckled and thrilled as they
watched. It was beyond the memory of any of them
the last time there had been hammer blows from
the plateau of Arnhor. And they wanted a closer
look. They wanted to see the young man himself.
Child Moxies did somersaults backwards and big
dark Moxies stretched out under all the shadows,
creeping closer and closer. No two of them alike,
for Moxies are magical creatures who can change
their shape at will. Right now there were Moxies
with horns on their heads, Moxies with foot-long
tongues hanging out, three-legged, five-legged
Moxies dancing. There was even an eye popper
among them — a rare oddity who could shoot her
eyeballs on elastic stalks almost three feet in either
direction, then bounce them back in with a *Gawp!*
One Moxie was so excited he peered right into the
fading light causing his nose to double, then triple
its size, before it popped and shrank and he hid
back away. Soon the night would be here and they
would be able to come right out and play! And still
the young man hammered away and sang at the
forge.

With each blow something took shape in his
hands, working away at the edge, delicately and pre-
cisely, driven by that high-up and deep-down voice
as he sang his spell-song. Something took shape.

"Hammer, hammer," he sang,

It's the song of the steel
In the soul of the shield,
And the same is the blow
On the steel in the soul.
Whatever shape you take,
You hammer, hammer, hammer your love
In the thing you make,
In the thing you make.

The sun was almost down now and the man suddenly began to double the pace of his hammering, shouting "Hammer! Hammer! Hammer!" with each blow, the fire burning hard, the anvil stone glowing like a small sun. And then he paused. Silence. He held up a sword, the blade close to his eyes, its tip still glowing with the heat of its making, and inspected it. Moxies held their breath in excitement, moving closer and closer. "Yes!" He took the hilt in both hands and swung it once, twice round, leaving two glowing circles of fire in the air. Then, stamping his right foot, he thrust the sword victoriously upward so that the glowing tip had the appearance for a moment of one more earthly star among the many stars that shone that night — and just then — right then — right at that moment, the last light of the setting sun shot through the last mountain cleft at the earth's edge and caught in its glow the tip of that sword. And just then, right then, at that same moment, the first light of the rising moon peeked out from the other side of the mountain and it too met that new-made sword tip so that all shone bright in sunlight, in moonlight, in

3

starlight, in forge light — all shone bright and brighter yet before the sun finally sank away and the blue moon reigned.

A Moxie could go mad with such moonlight. The eye popper whispered "Second moon in the month of June" and they all began to tumble and rave in silent ecstasy. The man swung the sword, twice, thrice more as it cooled, leaving strange syllables glowing and fading in the night air. At last, when the sword tip had ceased to glow, there in the full rounded light of the moon, he called out, "Mother! Mother! I think it's finished. Come and see. Mother!" And he was so excited he could barely resist jumping up and down and tumbling and raving and dancing himself.

2

First
Magic!

Not far away in a little beam of that same moonlight, the baby Princess Illia was awake, all alone in her bedroom, and she didn't like it. She was thinking of her mother's face, trying to get a feeling of peace to enter her, but it wasn't working.

Outside in the courtyard, Oolus the Fool was making faces at the King's elite guard as they drilled. But there was a dark and terrible mood among them as they turned and paced and presented their arms. Even Oolus could not make them laugh. "Left turn!" the sergeant-at-arms called and a thousand heels and pike hilts swivelled and hit the ground at once. "Forward *harch!*" *Tromp! Tromp!* Somewhere war drums were beating and there was a panic in the populace. War! War!

"Left turn!"

Just then Oolus might have heard Princess Illia cry out but the sergeant shouted "Halt!" in a loud imperial voice and she missed it.

Illia could not summon up her mother's picture in her mind. The room was feeling gigantic and she sensed the presence of powerful forces. Strange almost-faces formed and melted in the dim corners of the room. A giant laughing head seemed to leer out for a moment from her closet. "Maaaa!" she called — her one word — and this Oolus heard.

By now Illia was in a bit of a furor. She was, after all, a princess and she knew it. She expected better service than this. Where was her mother? She babbled in rage. "Ma-N-e-uglukn-ma-ma!" Then, just as Oolus entered the room, Queen Blue's image did appear, not only in Illia's mind but in her mirror, on the backs of her fingernails, in the bowl of water at her bedside — and outside about twelve feet high on the courtyard wall where the sergeant-at-arms and all the King's men were stunned into silence by the shimmering and beautiful apparition. Seeing her mother's serene face, that feeling of peace finally came over Illia.

"Queen Blue!" In a hushed voice Oolus fell to her knee and doffed her fool's cap.

While Illia chortled over what she had done, Queen Blue's startled image burbled, "Hello, my little Grimblee." Illia smiled the biggest gap-tooth baby smile any mother could ever long to see. She laughed right out loud in her high baby voice so that Queen Blue could not help but respond with a delighted and loving laugh of her own.

6

"But why have you called, Oolus? Is there some problem?"

Oolus's voice caught in her throat with a sudden hush. "Why did *I* call?"

Both paused.

"Ma'am, twas not *I* who called . . ."

Illia downright shouted with joy at the look on their faces.

"Illia?" her mother whispered.

"Illia has done it herself, Ma'am — by the light of yon moon," Oolus confirmed.

"Oh, she will be powerful, Oolus. I knew it."

"I knew it too, Ma'am. She's going to be a great and magical Queen some day."

"Maaa! Maaa!" shouted Illia, triumphantly raising her hands in the air as Oolus danced her around.

But just then the Queen's image began to fade. "But Oolus," the Queen called out. "Oolus, this could mean big trouble. She is ahead of time. Do as we discussed. We need a knight! A special knight." Just as she finished saying this a cloud passed over the moon, the room darkened and she was gone. "Maaa! Maaa!" shouted Illia, but her magic was done for the night.

"Oh come, come, my darling." Oolus comforted her. "We must tell the King. We need a knight!"

3

Oaves!

Outside the Moxies were at fever pitch. The old Crone was coming! They could sense it. The young man took one more swing with his new-made blade, and then she emerged from her cave in the mountains.

"What is it, Ogo?" his mother asked in a voice that was lilting and young, and the Moxies swooned to see her at last.

"What a beautiful old Crone!"

"I think it is done!" the young man said, barely able to contain his excitement. "Look — it is light." He whirled it around. "It is strong!" He clanged the hilt down so that it sounded like a bell against the anvil stone. "It has balance." He held it in his palm. "And it is sharp!" The Moxies gasped to hear the hiss as his sword cut through the night air. This was no ordinary swordsman!

8

"And it is dangerous," his mother admonished, taking the sword from him as with a gallant gesture he offered it to her.

"Yes, Mother."

The old woman continued. "This sword must be used with great care." She took it and balanced it in her palm. Then she held it up gently before the moon. "I see it does catch the light in a most mystical way."

"Have I succeeded then, Mother?"

"Yes, yes, there *is* magic in it."

"O Mother!"

"Yes, Ogo," she said, hugging him and then handing him back the sword. "I can feel wonderful things in it. One day it will be the envy of swords."

"The envy of swords!" Ogo almost sang. "O Mother, I am so happy. Now, I know I can face the Laughing Giant." Ogo struck a blow into the shadows. "And who knows? Maybe even dragons." Again he swung the blade. "Dragons, Mother. It is all I've ever dreamed of."

"Wasn't there one other dream?"

"Another?" he asked.

"Yes, son, since you were a child and you first saw the sunlight flashing on silver —"

"Well yes, I have dreamed of knighthood, but — that is impossible for a man not born of royal blood."

"Impossible?"

"Especially when you have no horse."

"Ogo, many things are possible when you wish and work for them."

"Well, I've wished and worked. And I do have some — uh — equipment."

"Yes you do, Ogo, and I know you must go soon to find your way in the world a while alone. But before you go with this powerful and dangerous sword I must ask one promise of you."

"Any promise, Mother. Ask it."

"Many long years you have lived with me in these caverns. I have raised you on the magical well water here, and I have fed you on the leaves and fruits of the earth about us. You have breathed the purest vales of earth-air and we have taken as we pleased and returned as we believed, moving the great wheel of magic around. Now, son, you have received from the earth this strange metal that you have shaped and the magic has moved to a higher plane. When you wield this sword it is more than just a sword. Remember that."

"Yes, Mother," Ogo replied a little impatiently.

"You must keep the movement of magic even in your swordplay — in the fiercest battles or in the richest peace you must never raise this sword against the earth. For it has come from the earth. And so, Ogo, I want you to swear the ancient oath before the Sky Gods, before the Goddess and the Moxies."

"Oaves! Oaves!" the Moxies shrilled, for Moxies love oaths. Suddenly the plateau was thick with Moxies. Unusually silent Moxies. "Hark. Hark."

Ogo knelt down on one knee, holding the new-born sword with both hands against his heart and spoke a verse that had come down to his people from ancient times.

Though far I roam in distant lands
From this hallowed place of birth,
No weapon shall I ever raise
Against our mother — Earth.

Ogo's mother nodded approvingly and the Moxies cheered.

"And now get a good night's rest, my son, for in the morning you will leave for Olliador." There was a sadness now in her voice. She gave Ogo a gentle kiss and returned into the dark curve of the cave. And there he stood under a blue moon in the midst of a pack of raving, ecstatic, dancing Moxies. Carefully so as not to tread on any of the little ones, Ogo did a little high-stepping dance of his own. "The envy of swords! The envy of swords!" he sang.

4

A Change
In Regulations

There was something a little silly about Vent as he strode along the mountain pathway next morning. He didn't always dance when he walked but just now he was singing a song, and there was something about the tune that gave his left leg a peculiar little leap at about every third step. Occasionally he did arm wiggles and head moves because he thought no one was watching him. But Vent was not alone on the mountain road that day. Someone was watching him. Someone was listening as he sang.

Oh I was born on a lucky day,
On a lucky day in the rain,
And every ever-come-after day
Was a lucky day again.
Oh here's to health and wealth (in my case),
Here's to freedom, I say,

Thanks to good fortune for coming my way,
Today is my lucky day.

Wiggling his hips a little and imagining an audi-
ence of enraptured young ladies, Vent approached
a very large boulder that stood by the side of the
road.

All that ever happened to me,
Though I mustered considerable pluck
And sometimes suffered in agony,
Eventually brought me good luck.
And so if I'm met with a setback,
If I'm down in the mire and the muck,
I know that even the worst things in life
Somehow just bring me good luck.

The watcher — a young man in dark armour and
a black mask — clutched a brand new axe-headed
staff tight in his hands and snickered as Vent performed a particularly silly chin movement.

And even bad luck turns to better
If I work it down to the good,
If I walk it down to the worthy
And face it down like I should.
My bad luck turns to better,
There's good luck inside the bad.
I'm glad 'cause I know bad luck might be
The best luck I've ever had.

No sooner had Vent finished this last verse than
the man in the black helmet leapt out from behind

the boulder, and gripping Vent tightly from behind about the chest with his staff, said, "Let's see how much good luck this brings ya."

Vent emitted a startled squeal. But he soon recovered as he had been trained to do and began trying unsuccessfully to flip his attacker over his head.

"Why, it is you, Fub!" he said angrily. "Stop now. Stop."

"Ha. Sure I'll stop," his attacker mocked him. "I'll stop like this!" Fub tapped fiercely on Vent's skull.

"Fub! Stop!" Vent yelled again.

"But how when you haven't seen me yet can you tell it's me, Vent?" Fub asked, releasing Vent and drawing his broadsword. "Is it the incredible power of my blows?" Fub rained a series of mighty blows upon Vent's sword.

"No!" Vent retorted angrily, parrying the blows with skill. "Now stop it."

"Aaah," the attacker continued. "Then it must be the signature hiss of my sizzling steel as it cuts through the air."

Fub swung wildly so that his sharp blade did actually hiss in the air. Vent ducked expertly.

"No, you vile bully," he shouted. "That's not what gives you away. It's that you play dirty." *Clang!* "It's that you come up from behind." *Clang! Clang!* "Who else would use such bully boy ways?" Fub lunged at Vent anew.

"Waaaaaaaa! Waaaaaaaa! Goo goo. Whaddaya gonna do — tell yer mommy?" Fub mocked. Now Vent got angry. Swinging wildly he caught Fub a solid blow right on the side of his head.

"Hey, watch it!" Fub complained, surprised.

"Is this your idea of psyching me out?" Vent asked sarcastically, beginning to regain a little confidence as Fub flailed uselessly away at him, unable to beat down his well-trained defence.

"No, this is my idea of —" *Clang!* "— rubbing you out. Smidgen." Fub emphasized his words with truly mighty blows.

"You always limit your opponents." Vent reeled beneath these blows, beginning to be out of breath.

"You speak like someone about to make an excuse —" *Clang!* "— for losing. Ha ha."

"I speak the truth. You chose me for this bout just as you chose that pipsqueak Sunderling, and Egast and Epplplock and all the others —"

"Ooo-Hoo. Testy today, aren't we? Grasping a straw when a broadsword won't work." *Clang!* "Down, you beaten thing. Even your armour is weak. Look." *Clang!* "It gives like a saucepan on a little boy's head." *Clang!* Fub brought his face right up close to Vent's and said, "I have the strongest armour."

"The strongest breath, maybe!" *Clang!*

And so the two young men continued their rather unequal bout, one the better with words and the other the better with a sword.

Higher up the mountain Ogo had begun his journey. More of his people than he had ever seen before at once came out from their shadow places and stood about him on the plateau. Not only his mother but his grandmother and great-grandmother were there, and there was much well-wishing and

15

a little weeping. The elders embraced him one by one, holding his face close, warmly cheek to cheek as is the manner of his people. And some gave him herbs to take with him, and some gave him messages for friends in the world down below. His grandmother, whom they say was part Moxie, gave him a tiny little book of Moxie lore and his great-grandmother gave him a smooth lodestone — a stone from the original home of their people 10,000 years in the past.

Finally, Ogo had said his goodbyes. Slowly he walked off the rim of the plateau and began his way down the blue stone road. He had not gone far when he heard the sounds of two men fighting.

There was more anger now in Fub's blows. He was the mightier. Why didn't Vent just accept that he was beaten? Why fight on when the end was inevitable? Just as he was thinking this Fub was upended by a very skillful tripping kick which Vent had learned last term at school. Enraged, Fub found himself sprawled on the ground.

Now, in a real battle, an experienced warrior would quickly have put his blade at Fub's throat and called for him to yield, but Vent hesitated just long enough for Fub to roll sideways and hurl his staff so that the flat blunt end of it struck Vent soundly on the forehead. Fub leapt up from the ground, scooted behind the staggering Vent and drove his knees forward into the back of Vent's knees all the while pinioning his arms. Down went Vent face forward into the dust. And this was when Ogo, quietly and unobserved, arrived. Fub put one

16

foot against Vent's lower back, pulled his long red hair from behind and attempted to say, "Yield." What came out was "Ye-ee-hee-hee-hee-eee." Fub was laughing. Fub was having a good time.

"I yield, I yield!" Vent had to shriek angrily before Fub would let him go.

"Well learned, Vent," said Fub, helping Vent up from the ground. "I do hope you will thank me for this timely lesson."

"Yes — it's always nice to get some practice dealing with ambush and despicable tactics," Vent responded bitterly.

"Hey come on, Ventsy," said Fub. "It was just a play fight. What was that about me limiting my opponents? I've fought every young lord in the district."

"Yes, you've fought all the lords, my tricky one, but what of all the commoners?"

Ogo now stood behind the same boulder where Fub had waited earlier.

"Commoners!" spat Fub. "They have no swords. No shields! How could I fight them?"

"O come on — what about Ogo, that smith's boy in Lightswich?"

"You mean the big potato-faced chap — the old Crone's son?"

Ogo's jaw tightened when he heard this.

"Many call him handsome," said Vent.

"A pretty face won't stop a broadsword, my friend."

"So you're saying you could beat him."

"I don't have to say anything. I will not be contesting with him. He's a commoner. There happens

17

to be a social order based on this stuff, Ventsy. Or hadn't you noticed?"

"He's twice as strong as you," Vent continued enthusiastically. "I saw him lift the Alvrazon-boulder to help a little child retrieve a marble."

"Well, I'm not going out to fight some common garden potato just because he's a good schoolie."

Ogo grimaced fiercely. Lord or no lord, he was not going to let these insults go by unchallenged. Finding the hilt of his sword he moved to step forward, but just then there was a trumpet blast.

"Hear ye, hear ye," the Royal Barker called, spying Vent and Fub. "Perk up all young athletes, brave young men, wise young men, agile young men of any stock. Unusual news from the capital. Due to increased demand there will be a surprise competition beginning tomorrow to find young men eligible for knighthood."

"Knighthood! Oh excellent. I thought we'd have to wait another whole year," Vent burbled.

"Attention, please," the Barker continued. "Let it be known also that there has been a change in the regulations. This is a special competition and is open to *all* young men who want to become knights — even commoners. Whoever is the most agile. Whoever is the best. The search is on for a knight. A special knight. A knight of any birth anywhere. Let him dart to the King and take on a quest."

Ogo could hardly believe his ears. Fast as he could run he headed toward the palace at Rhun with great joy in his heart.

"Well, now I *will* thank you for attacking me, Fub," Vent chortled, not noticing Ogo. "I was just

19

on my way back to school. You see — my bad luck did turn to good. If you hadn't ambushed me like that I'd have been on my way and missed this announcement."

"Well, let's just see how your luck holds in the contests."

"And let's just see how you do against . . . commoners."

"Strange concept. The King must have something up his sleeve."

"Yes, arms I think!"

"I wonder if he's been taking advice from his Fool again."

So saying, the two of them headed off down the blue road to the King's court.

5

Arms
and Charms

Swords for sale! Get your good brass swords right here!" The arms merchants were full of daring today. They could almost smell the war in the wind. "Shields for sale!" they called. "Get your dirks sharpened." Business had been very good lately. Here they were not two blocks from the palace and no one to say Nay! Stealthily, as they unfolded their valises into small tables upon which to display their wares, they chatted among themselves.

"It's looking good for war," Gimble burbled, rubbing his hands gleefully together.

"Yes." Flam the importer positioned his collection of dirks artfully about the table. "I thought the bloody peace was gonna last forever."

"Still, we can't be overconfident," said Marg, the charms merchant. "They say the King will do his best to avoid a fight."

"Well, even the threat of a fight is good for business," Flam advised as he started to remove the latest in weaponry from his voluminous robes.

"Yes, yes, sell now and hope for the worst." They laughed grimly.

"To the worst!" said Flam, holding up his flask.

"The worst!" the other two chimed in, chinking their flasks and taking long sweet quaffs.

"It is a funny time when the worst is the best we can hope for," Flam wheezed.

"That's how it goes in a kingdom that is run by the King's Fool," said Marg.

"Yes, hail this great century of the idiot," Gimble quipped, taking another long draw on his flask, "when you can't tell the difference between government and a bloody joke."

"I love this new joke," Flam laughed, as he put the finishing touches on his dirk display, "to admit even commoners into the competitions for knighthood."

"All the more business for us," said Marg, rubbing her hands gleefully together again.

"Yes, here's to Oolus, then," said Gimble, holding up his flask again for a toast.

"To Oolus the Fool, for she keeps us all employed!" they toasted, and all had a deep, intoxicating quaff.

"Ready, fellows," Marg warned, "here they come." Marg had spotted a rather unusual looking fellow coming toward them. Unusual in that his armour had a strange sheen and shape to it and he was walking very fast.

"O sir. Careful now. These are dangerous times.

22

Have a care," Flam warned as Ogo approached. "You have but flimsy armour on your back. Beware, mein herr. Beware." As he said this, Flam did a most rude thing: he tapped lightly on Ogo's armour with the brass sword he had been waving about. "Get my new anti-knight spray," he called, offering Ogo a bottle with a nozzle atop it. "Just spray those bad guys away." But Ogo refused the bottle and tried to walk by.

"It works immediately," Flam persisted, blocking the way. "Look, look, sir, as I spray it on this hard brass sword. Look, sir, see how solid it is?" Flam gave the sword a good strong swat against Ogo's armour. Before Ogo could object, Flam pressed the nozzle on top of the bottle so that mist shot from it with a loud hiss. Immediately the brass sword began to wilt as though it were a fainting flower. "See. See how it wilts," Flam barked excitedly. "Just spray those bad guys away. Your enemies won't stand a chance!"

"That's disgusting," Ogo said, trying to push past, but Flam was persistent. "But look, you, chappy, look." He grabbed Ogo's shoulder so that Ogo had to turn and face him again. "How brilliant we are. Not only do we have the anti-knight spray, but look." Marg held up another spray can. "Anti-anti-knight spray. Just spray some of this on your own sword and look — no anti-knight spray can harm you." Flam took up another sword, sprayed it first with the anti-anti-knight spray, and then sprayed the anti-knight spray on it. This time the sword did not wilt. To prove this Flam gave another good solid swat against Ogo's armour, causing

Ogo to clench his fists in anger. He responded with one simple but firm syllable: "No."

"Now isn't he on a high horse!" said Flam as Ogo proceeded on his way.

"So high you can't see it," said Marg.

"He's not a royal anyway," Gimble said.

"Just a commoner," said Flam the commoner, with considerable distaste. "Encouraged by the King's Fool-ish plan to let anybody in."

"I don't care if he's common or not," Gimble said, taking another long swig on his flask, "as long as he buys. A sale is a sale and without a sucker there's no sale."

"Well, I just hope some real suckers come along soon," replied Flam. Just then, who should come around the corner but Vent and Fub.

"Hey — Cannon! Cannon for sale!" Gimble shouted eagerly. "Look, you young lads. Are you sick of having to get close to your enemy? Look, look at this new weapon." Gimble held up what appeared to be a black top hat. "It looks like a simple gentleman's hat, boys, but really its a small, portable, disposable cannon. Just think of it — a long-range weapon you can wear on your head." Gimble put the black hat on his head and struck what he thought to be a devilish pose. "And it looks good too! All made out of strong iron and powered by powder." Then Gimble removed the hat with a gallant sweep and placed it on the ground so that leaning on the brim it aimed upwards like a small sawed-off cannon. "Able to send blunt heavy missiles hurtling through space and pick out a target miles away. You never even have to see their faces!"

"Uh, no thanks," Vent answered, hurrying by. "Those are most unlucky instruments, I think. But what are these?" He made his way to Marg's 'table of fortune' where all manner of lucky dice, rabbit's feet and medallions were on display. "Amazing — triple-sided playing cards!" he sighed.

"Why, you're very lucky, sir," said Marg. "That's the very last pack I have left. And look at these diamond dice, good sir," she continued, talking conspiratorially to Vent. "Ninety-sided dice only the truly lucky can roll." Vent hesitated. "Of course," she wheedled, "a gentleman might rather have one of these simple but elegant medallions." She held up a small silver disk on which a figure of the Goddess Diana had been embossed.

"Why, that's my lady!" Vent burbled. "Why, this is good luck indeed." So saying, he purchased not only a medallion but the dice and playing cards as well before continuing on his way.

By now Flam had sized up Fub, who had been watching all this with a grim face.

"Sire," Flam began obsequiously, "you look like a man who is not afraid to dispatch an enemy quickly. Look — why fool around with a common heavy hand-moved broadsword? Look at this baby — sir." With that he pulled from within the folds of his tattered cloak a strange-looking sword with a small string dangling from the hilt. "An import, sir — straight from Helliconia. Completely safe and environmental. It runs on body heat. The new automatic chainsword." Flam gave a yank to the string at the end of the hilt. Zzzzz! The sword began to

25

whir and buzz as a chain of spikes and points rotated around the edge of the blade.

Fub was truly impressed, but he knew enough to hide this from the salesman. He wanted the best deal possible.

"Oh yes, very gallant," he responded dryly, taking the sword in hand and giving it a bored buzzing wave through the air. "But at what price?" Zzzzzz! went the sword with a sound like a thousand flies.

"Sire, for you," said Flam, "a mere twelve drachmas."

"Oh come now," Fub spat. "Do you take me for some kind of bumpkin?"

"Okay, Okay. I can see you're a fellow with some destiny about him," Flam gabbed his sales pitch. "I'll tell you what. I'm in a crazy, generous mood. Let me make a special deal. Buy one of these electric chainswords at the regular price and I'll throw in one of these disposable pocket cannon hats at no extra cost."

"Disposable?"

"Use it once and throw it away. No costly cartage. No messy clean-up."

"Enchanting," Fub said sarcastically, as though uninterested. He picked up the hat, sniffed it gingerly and plopped it back down on the table with apparent disgust. Then he made as if to put the sword down too, but Flam was getting close and he knew it. "Plus," he barked, holding up one finger, "I'll throw in this complete set of stainless steel daggers and dirks worth over nine drachmas. And that's not all. If you buy right now —" But just then a most disgusted look came over Fub's face. Fub had an idea.

26

"Why, you scoundrels," he shouted, giving a good strong tug on the chainsword so that it began to buzz and whir and vibrate in his hands. Zzzzzzzzz! "Don't you know that automatic weapons have been officially frowned on by the King?"

The arms merchants sputtered and protested, but when they drew near to Fub he waved the chainsword at them, cutting the legs off their tables. "Off, off with you!" he screamed.

"Scum! Filth!" they shouted back, enraged. "A curse on you. May weasels stomp your blood!" But they were helpless. Fub was a lord and they were nobodies. Fub affixed the combination scabbard and recharge unit around his waist, grabbed a few cans of anti-knight spray, placed the cannon hat on his head and sauntered away with a laugh.

6

No
Horse

Standing at the gate of the King's palace, Ogo was amazed. He had never seen Paper People before and he couldn't help staring. Seven of them in a row, four of them decorated with hearts and three with diamonds, stood in sullen majesty, their long tin trumpets held primly at their sides. Every once in a while some visiting dignitary would enter the palace. Whenever this happened, which was often, as these dignitaries appeared to like nothing better than causing a big stir, the Paper People would flip up their horns as one, take a big breast-doubling breath and blow exhilarating harmonies, titanic fanfares that shook the very ground you stood on. Ogo felt his armour vibrate with the sound and longed to play one of the horns himself.

Finally a strange little figure in a three-cornered fool's cap half-danced, half-capered toward Ogo across the courtyard to survey him up and down with a sniff. "Here for quests?" the figure asked finally.

"Yes."

"Yes, you have the smell of a Quester."

"I see," Ogo replied cautiously.

"Are you man or Moxie?"

"Why, a man!" said Ogo. ". . . mostly."

"Mostly a man?" the Fool asked.

"I *am* a little bit Moxie," Ogo admitted a little proudly. The Fool sniffed again — a good deep sniff.

"Yah!" she said. "Well, Moxie-man, man or Moxie, Moxie or man or all of the above — you wait over there in the stables with your . . . horse." Ogo headed toward the distant building she pointed to, even though he did not have a horse.

Alone in the waiting room, which was in the stables, Ogo paced up and down nervously. Soon. Soon he would get a quest. The more he thought about it, the happier and more excited he became. As usual, being a playful fellow, he began to daydream about the trials to come. He imagined the dignified way in which he would win all the contests, impressing all, not only with his strength and cunning but with his graciousness and courtesy in winning. As he fantasized, Ogo's hand drifted to his sword hilt and without thinking he drew it with one deft tug from its scabbard and began to hack and hew at the air with it, as though he were already in battle. In the middle of this, Vent and Fub entered the room. Fub snickered.

"And who might you be, Sir Swordsman?"

"My name is — "

"Ogo!" Vent said enthusiastically. "This is —"

"Oh yes," Fub interrupted, "the *commoner*. Uh huh. And I suppose you're here as part of this sort of temporary let-anybody-in thing."

"That's right." Ogo found himself disliking Fub intensely. "I want to, uh, get in."

"Fat chance!" Fub snorted.

"I think the King is showing great leadership in making these changes," said Vent as he and Fub tied up their horses.

"Anyway," Fub eyed Ogo's armour with a look of great disapproval. "I'm Cornelius Hoophus RubFubbis Fubson McDango El Fub dePhubson." He said his name as though it were a fanfare and ought to bring Ogo to his knees.

"I know, Fub," said Ogo.

"My father was a commander at Vantannalay."

Again Ogo was not impressed. "I know."

"I'm going to follow in his footsteps and earn my knighthood with a good first conquering." Fub brought his face closer to Ogo's. "Fub the Conqueror. Yes."

"Personally I'm hoping for something a little less bloodthirsty," Vent said, parting them with his hands. "If I'm lucky I'll be asked to retrieve some fabulous item from some distant, preferably romantic region. It's fairly standard. Something with a princess involved would suit me entirely. Perhaps the marrying kind, if you know what I mean." By now three other young men had entered the room and were quietly grooming their horses, listening to the conversation.

"What about you, Ogo? How would you like to earn your knighthood?" Vent asked.

"Recently herds of dragons have been spotted about the steel mills," Ogo said quietly. "I wouldn't mind cleaning them up a little."

"Sir Ogo of Dragons," mocked Fub with a wink to the three new men. "I don't know if dragons fight commoners."

"Actually they only fight un-commoners when you think about it," Vent interjected. "Not many people get to fight a dragon. And this Ogo here looks like a very un-common chap to me."

"On the other hand," Ogo continued, "I have a deep, deep anger against the Laughing Giant, who has humiliated so many of our proudest knights."

Fub rolled his eyes at the three men.

"Sir Ogo of Giants," Vent said. "It has a good ring about it."

"If I could just have a chance," Ogo spoke earnestly, "I would gladly risk everything to defeat that menace."

"But tell us, Ogo," and again Fub began to move in close to Ogo, "I understand that you have used your initiative and, uh, some book learning to overcome some of the disadvantages of being, uh, low-born."

"If being born quite close to Mother Earth means being low-born," Ogo responded a little loudly, "then you are right. I am low-born. And I live a low life too."

"Well, I guess it takes all parts of a barrel to hold water," Fub quipped, and one of the men laughed out loud. "Now I understand you've used a do-it-yourself guide to teach yourself swordsmanship and, uh, etiquette." Fub fed his horse a handful of grain.

"Correct," Ogo bristled.

"And you've actually learned blacksmithing from your mother." Now all three of the men laughed. "And made your own armour and sword et al."

Ogo felt his temper rise at this jibe but he answered in a very calm way. "That's right." Several more young men now entered the room, among them a fellow named Welwin, who was also a commoner.

"But tell us, dear Ogo. All these things can be made or learned at little or no cost and with no connections. But what of a horse, may I ask?"

"Aaah, a horse." Fub had Ogo and he knew it.

"You can't *make* a horse. Can you now, Ogo?" Fub persisted.

"That's right, Ogo," Vent agreed. "What do you do for a horse?"

"As yet I have no horse."

As one, Fub and Vent and some of the other men protested. "No horse! A knight with no horse! As yet! How? How?"

"You are quite right to point out that I can make no horse," Ogo said quietly.

"Exactly." Fub sensed victory.

"So for now," Ogo went on, "I have no horse."

"But how will you get to these dragons and giants and such which you so ardently seek to do battle with?"

Ogo replied simply. "One day soon I have faith I will have a horse."

32

"How could you possibly purchase a horse?" said Fub, and again his voice was full of lordly contempt.

Ogo's answer was almost a whisper. "A wild horse!"

"A wild horse!" Fub laughed right in Ogo's face. "But how will you catch it, pray tell Ogo? You can't catch a horse *without* a horse."

"I can catch it," Ogo retorted quietly and severely. "Though I was not born with royal blood like you, sir, I was lucky enough to have been born with a good healthy body and some degree of common speed."

"Oh I see — and you can outrun a horse, I suppose."

"He can," Vent confirmed excitedly. "You should see him. He can throw a ball full-tilt and then run and catch it before it lands." Several of the men tittered at this.

"Oh twaddle," said Fub.

Ogo's voice was decidedly hard and angry as he turned on Fub. "You keep citing your royal blood. But what do you think? Maybe having royal blood just makes you a *royal* pain in the —"

Who knows how Ogo might have finished this sentence, for just then the stable door flew open and in walked the funny little person in the three-cornered hat. Ogo and Fub glared at one another but were silent as Oolus spoke. "All right, lardies, your fate is here. Come with me."

33

7

The Fool's
New Rules

Ogo had seen many mysteries of the mineral in his home inside the mountain. He had journeyed deep into underground canyons and far along the crystal shafts of Urth. But nothing had prepared him for this vision of the high court at Olliador. Here, as in myths, sat the Ruby Throne, crested high with its spiral of diamonds and gold. Everywhere, as though hewn from gigantic rubies, were pillars, horns, sceptres and towers. Here where the sun set in the West, here in Worldcleft Castle, through rubylight the young men walked, led by the attendant. Seeing them, the trumpet masters raised their horns as though to blow a fanfare, but when they found out it was only an attendant and some young men, they returned their horns stiffly to their sides and grimaced and scowled.

No one in the court that morning was feeling the least bit light-hearted. There was a shortage of beets, the price of rice was high and last night there had been rumours that Queen Blue had appeared in a vision to the King and had prophesied either a Day of Endless Night or a Night of Endless Day. Or that she had called for a Night to come upon them.

After much waiting, during which time the young men shuffled from foot to foot, silently, the trumpeters raised their horns and unleashed the single longest fanfare Ogo had ever heard. "Lords and ladies!" someone yelled. "Young men! Everybody — the KING!"

Ogo was surprised to see the man who then emerged at the top of the staircase. He had been expecting the grandiose lion of a man depicted on the coins of Olliador. But this king had cut off his long mane, shaved his flowing beard and moustache and now appeared close-cropped and bare-headed, except for two startling and lamb-choppy sideburns. There was still, however, a great amount of authority in his face, and a kind of warmth exuded from him that instantly calmed many of them. Ogo felt it deep in his gut — a desire to be loyal to this man, a desire to submit in fealty and receive his trial and tempering.

Now another titanic fanfare was sounded. "All rise for the Princess Illia!" If the court's bleak mood had been lightened by the appearance of the King, it was absolutely levitated by the arrival of the Princess Illia. Held high in Oolus's arms she let loose her largest, most infectious smile and immediately performed the only royal duty she knew as

35

yet. She began to wave. Delighted, her favourites at court waved back. And then the King began to wave too, so more members of the court waved back, and then everybody waved. All the while Princess Illia, Oolus, and the King descended the spiral staircase to the court.

When they reached the bottom there was a moment of complete silence and then Illia said something which sounded like, "Ma go guugullua!"

"Aaah! Duck! Hit the deck!" Oolus the Fool screamed in a truly nerve-shattering voice. Immediately the King and all the worried courtiers and attendants and men-at-arms and ladies-in-waiting all dove as one to the floor, holding their hands over their heads as the court astrologer frantically thumbed through a very large and magical looking book, spelling out loud as he did so.

"M-a-g-o-g-u-u-g-u-" And all the time Illia in her father's arms crouched on the floor and giggled.

"Oh! Oh!" said the astrologer, sounding relieved. "A double-U! It's okay. All's well."

"You may rise now." Cautiously the floor-hugging court slowly rose, some of them still looking nervously about as though some kind of invasion or miraculous attack were about to happen.

"I'm sorry, Sire," Oolus said. "I thought she said . . ." Oolus whispered in the King's ear so that none might hear the magical syllables. Then aloud to all she added with a shrug of her comical shoulders, "I just thought better safe than sorry!"

"Quite right, Oolus," the King confirmed patiently. His voice was rich and golden. "Uh, perhaps I'd better explain." He turned to the still shaken court. "Illia's mother, Queen Blue, as you know, has magic powers. Illia will soon speak her first words, and due to an incident which occurred last night there is some fear that she might accidentally unleash powerful spells — turning people into pumpkins — that sort of stuff. So our royal astrologer here has been charged to look up any of her babblings in his compendium of spells and antidotes in order that we might avoid or correct any, uh, accidental havoc." Here he gave his daughter a gentle little tickle under the chin. She piped up, "Ma-go gguguli!" and again half the court ducked nervously, some holding their hands over their heads. Seeing what an effect she had, Illia let loose a baby laugh, high and musical and uncontained.

"She's such a caution!" Oolus chortled.

"Well," said the King, eyeing her with affection and amusement, "we'd better get on with the task at hand. I see a rather large assortment of young men before me who are here no doubt in response to the good news which I have caused to be known about changes in regulation regarding knighthood. For the first time in history the lists for knighthood are open to all men. Birthright shall no longer yield the only way in. We can no longer exclude strength from our ranks. Nor intelligence. Nor is this the only change in regulations. Oolus, perhaps you'd better tell them."

"Hello lads, my name is Oolus." Oolus posed with exaggerated majesty beside the Ruby Throne. "Many of you know me, or have heard of me, as the King's Fool."

Some of the young men who had been at court before laughed, thinking they were about to hear one of Oolus's idiot sermons.

"However," continued Oolus, "the real joke is that I'm also His Majesty's official minister of state, his military advisor and prime minister." Oolus took a bow, and all laughed, so that she jerked back up with an angry shout.

"Right now I am being the prime minister."

"Oh!" The men tried to control their laughter as Oolus glared fiercely at them.

In a decidedly prime ministerial voice she continued. "His Majesty, as you have heard, is open to all manner of changes in the way things are run. You will be happy to know that he has given the go-ahead for me to change the tourneys." Here, Oolus held up her hand as though for great cheers, but none came.

"Hmmmm. You see, warfare is changing. There are new methods, new weapons. And what was once settled with force and bloodshed is lately being settled by other means. Initially, as we winnow you men out, you shall contest in the normal ways — jousting, ball and chain twirling, spear chucking, uh, axe throwing, sword play and, uh, pig chucking. But when three finalists are found, there will be a further new contest to determine the overall winner and to assign quests. Good luck to . . . the pluckiest. Let the games begin!"

8

The Games

And so the next day, the many men who had come to take on a quest contested amongst themselves. Some of them wrestled and some of them ran and all of them tried the bow and a few were chosen to find wild roots and barks and berries and make of them a meal and some were daubed with colours and sent into the forest to hijack certain hidden scarecrows and bring them back "alive."

Although they had come from all the regions of Olliador most of these men as usual were nobility — cultured, well-trained, wealthy young men. Ogo's prowess and strength soon became legend among them, but few welcomed him into their ranks, for he was a commoner. Indeed, led on by the scurrilous Fub, they had taken to calling him Ogers or Uggo or worse yet — Potato! But Ogo bore this resolutely, a mountain in their midst.

By the second day of the tourney people had arrived from far and wide to watch the games. The crowd was huge. There was the local populace, the knights and their retinues, visiting princes, ambassadors and businessmen, young ladies and defeated candidates. And everywhere, everywhere, the local children were rooting for Fub! They didn't notice Ogo the Commoner. It was Fub! Fub! Fub! The glorious Fub. The almighty Fub. Fub the Conqueror. For Fub had easily established himself as a winner amongst them. Fub the wrestler. Nutcracker Fub the cudgel man. Dancing Fub the kick-boxer. Fub — the toppler, the tripper, the gripper, the jousting, jumping, jubilant, thumping Fub. Every contest he entered Fub won. It's true one of his opponents had a peculiar accident which caused his sword to wilt, but no one doubted that Fub would have won that match anyway. Certainly not the increasing hordes of children who adored the black-hooded Fub and shouted "Fub! Fub! Fub! Fub!" whenever he strode onto the field.

Ogo longed to take on Fub. But luck was against him. Always he drew a different contest or a different contestant. And though he too won every one of his contests nobody seemed to notice. Slowly, though, the candidates were being eliminated and sooner or later, Ogo knew he would have his chance at this prancing and glorious Fub.

Finally there were but six men left. Not till then did the Fool call an actual sword fight. But before she let it begin she brought the men together and made them embrace and drink toasts to one another and swear friendship.

Strange to see Ogo and Fub eye to eye, touching hands for the first time, swearing friendship. And Vent too, who'd shown an unusual prowess at wrestling and an amazing virtuosity and good fortune with the long bow. No fool, this Vent. He could pierce the heart of a cherry at a hundred yards. And even when his arrows were off, it was said, the wind blessed him and blew them straight.

Despite his reputed luckiness, when the time came to draw lots for the sword fights, Vent drew the fiercest swordsman of them all — Melvin Axmaster, a quite gigantic Tornkian from the far coast who was rumoured to have killed a man once.

Fub drew Jem Ferrames. Jem the Gem — likewise a giant of a man and likewise undefeated. Ogo had been praying for a chance to take on Fub but he drew instead Welwin Greene, a fellow whom he rather liked and the only other commoner in the fight.

Watching the giant Axmaster whirl his scimitar in practice for the fight, it was difficult for Vent to maintain faith in his good luck. Over and over he rubbed his Diana medallion and sang in his head, "Even bad luck turns to better if I work it down to the good." But it was hard to see how there could be anything lucky about this fight.

But, just as Vent finally stood before the towering Axmaster, just as Axmaster raised that shining scimitar high over Vent's terrified head, a horseman galloped onto the field. "Sire! Sire!" he called desperately, and Axmaster paused. Breathlessly the horseman imparted the news that Axmaster's father who had long been ill was about to die, and

41

had ordered his son home. Grief-stricken, the mighty Axmaster dropped his scimitar to his side, bowed courteously to Vent and departed immediately. Vent stood there, alone and relieved, in the middle of the arena, hardly realizing how well his luck had held again. For the judges had reached the only decision possible — Vent was declared the winner by default!

Meanwhile Ogo was sizing up Welwin Greene. He had heard that he was a fierce fighter, but now he could see that his arms were not wide and well-muscled and his legs were not deft and dancing. There was no great girth to his chest and really he didn't look that intelligent. Worst of all was his armour, which was very crudely made and had obviously been gathered from various unmatching sources, including several saucepan lids. Even as he made these judgements Ogo felt goodwill toward the man, and having determined that he could defeat him with speed and ease, he decided instead to take it a lot slower so that the fellow wouldn't lose face.

To Ogo's surprise, however, Welwin, after shaking hands and swearing friendship, came in with a short jab and nearly knocked Ogo off his feet, but Ogo lunged at the last minute, saving himself. Instantly Welwin was back at him and Ogo nearly fell again. CLASH! Before he could grab his own sword Welwin came swinging at him with a speed he had never faced in a fight before. Ogo rolled, his heart thumped, half-thrill, half-fright, and then he was up — way up, turning right round in the air, coming down, sword up, face on to Welwin. "Haw"

42

Welwin charged at Ogo and now they began with great energy (and many *clangs*) to have it out, blow upon blow, for an hour, full-tilt, with many a thrilling setback, many a near fall, many a death-defying thrust. It was the battle of the century, yet nobody but the referees watched. Everyone else was over at Potter's Field watching the fabulous Fub fight Ferrames.

Fub was not having a good day. His legion of fans had long since grown hoarse yelling "Fub! Fub! Fub!" and Ferrames still stood full of energy and smiling before him. "I'm gonna drub you, Fub. I'm gonna rub you, Fub. I'm gonna thrash you, Fub! I'm gonna scrub you, Fub!" Unfortunately this was not all talk. Fub's expensive armour had stood up well to the battering he was receiving, but Ferrames was obviously a much stronger and apparently a much more skilled swordsman. Slowly, deliberately, he beat Fub into his final corner and was about to finish him off. Many of the boys turned away bitterly, unable to watch. But then, suddenly — *Zzzzing!* Something happened. Ferrames leapt back with a yell and there was a great rend in his shield where Fub must have struck him a mighty blow. And there must have been a great swarm of bees or flies just then, for everybody heard the strange *Zzzzz* which filled the air. *Zzzzzing! Zzzzzang!* Fub was back! Fub struck! Fub stung! Making every blow count. What accuracy! What skill — even his smallest slash seemed to leave a mark wherever it touched. Even in Ferrames's sword. *Zzzzzing! Zzzzzang!*

43

Fub hacked and hewed and slashed and laughed as little bits of Ferrames's armour came flying off. The boys were all shouting so fiercely now that hardly anyone heard Ferrames's enraged protests. Courageously he kept coming at Fub, but it was no good. *Zzzzzzap! Zzzzzing!* Fub just kept on hacking and carving until with one deft swing he completely severed Ferrames's sword at the hilt. Not till then did the horde of flies or bees or whatever it was that was making that buzzing noise desist. "Fub! Fub! Fub!" the whole crowd was yelling. "Fub! Fub! Fub!" For Fub had won again.

9

A New Contest

I am pleased to announce," said the King, "that three finalists have emerged from our contests. These are . . . Please stand up . . . Vent Pomandler." Vent stood up tall and proud and several people who had seen his lucky shot with the bow applauded. "Cornelius Hoophus RubFubbis Fubson McDango El Fub dePhubson." Fub did not just stand up calmly in a dignified way as Vent had done. He leapt up from his knees, with his hands clutched victoriously over his head and his legs pumping up and down in a victory dance. The assembled courtiers and boys applauded loudly and even cheered until the King's gentle "Ahem!" silenced them. "And a fellow," he went on, "who breaks new ground among us, for he is the first commoner ever to join our competition. Ogo McJones." Ogo too felt a rush of joy. He had fought valiantly and courteously in the tournaments and he knew it. He couldn't help it: he held one hand theatrically high over his head, expecting his own cheer from the assembled masses, but none came. Ogo the commoner. Somewhere someone dropped a pot so that there was only a kind of tinny tink which caused Fub to snicker.

"I know I have before me," the King proceeded, "three mighty contenders, and it remains but to see who shall get which quest. So fellows, knowing you are all highly capable soldiers who might well one day be bonded with us in knighthood, Oolus here has devised a contest which shall call upon all your arts without setting you one against the other. Oolus, perhaps you'd like to tell them."

"Why squirtainly, yer amnesty." Oolus gave a funny little bum waddle as she spoke so that several of the courtiers laughed out loud. "Okay, lads, you have already proved yourself with great meat and stinky to be fit for battle in a physical way. But His Majesty asks — how are your souls?" And here it must be said that Fub, without thinking, took a surreptitious peek at the bottoms of his shoes. "How is your sense of invention, magic, timing?" Oolus went up to each of the three men and eyed them closely as she spoke. "Any true warrior must also be a poet. Therefore, in celebration of Princess Illia's upcoming birthday, you shall each be required to compose a poem for her."

Vent was delighted. "Poetry!" he exclaimed, clapping his hands together. Ogo too was pleased. "Poetry!" But not so Fub. "Poetry?" he muttered with contempt. Ignoring this, Oolus wheeled over a most majestic looking chest all encrusted with jewels and musical notes and strange magical looking designs. "I want each of you to reach into the Princess's toy box," she said, "and take out one item. Your poem must be about this item."

"Sire, who shall judge these . . . poems?" Fub asked.

"Why, if the poems are for Illia, then only she must judge. Isn't that right, my little judgee?" the King said. Illia gave her sweetest baby smile and answered, "Horg!"

"Yes. Exactly," replied the King. "Now each of you take one item."

Fub was first. The drums rolled, he turned his face away, reached deep into the chest and withdrew a small, stuffed, fluffy looking animal.

"A sheep!" he said, a little contemptuously.

Vent was next. Again the drums rolled. Vent covered his eyes with one hand, reached into the box with the other and withdrew something that to an inexperienced eye might have looked like rags and buttons bunched together in the middle with a piece of string. But when you turned it the right way round it was — "A doll!" Vent exclaimed. Illia, seeing the toy, called out "Gow! Gow!" and the scribes scribbled, but no one ducked.

Finally it was Ogo's turn. As the drum rolled he reached deep into the toy box until his hand brushed against something rough and hard. He held it up in the air and the crowd laughed. "A rock?" Ogo asked incredulously.

"Gow!" Illia responded gleefully.

"Uh yes, Gow!" laughed the King.

And so were the three topics of poetry chosen. Each man stood holding his toy urgently and nervously.

"Okay, Vent," Oolus said, "you're first."

"Why thank you, Ma'am." Vent responded with a gallant doff of his hat. "And I really do hope I haven't caught these others at a disadvantage. You see, I have a degree in poetry."

The King winked and whispered to Oolus, "He's also chosen her favourite toy in the world. How can he fail?" Then, louder, he said, "Ready, Vent?"

A most serious, even pained look came over Vent's features.

"Ready," he answered solemnly. And suddenly the court was completely silent. The pained look on Vent's face deepened and with a rather awkward flourish of one arm he began to recite.

Deep

And his voice deepened as he uttered the word.

in obdurate day,

He spoke, slowly, as though tasting each syllable, as though each word had an extra meaning beyond the normal meaning and only his pained and awkward writhing could somehow fully express that meaning.

Sun-heavy [grimace]
But light with *play* [finger tango]
An *effigy* — the hand dances,
Graceful,

48

With the word "graceful" Vent's voice almost broke with emotion so that everyone began to wonder if he were about to cry. But he recovered and continued.

I *name* you graceful . . .

Pause. Vent kind of hovered in the air before them, waiting for some final and awesome insight. Pause. Finally he finished the stanza with the obvious syllable:

Doll.

But he said it in such a way and with such a strange, passionate, weird look on his face that everyone wondered if there were perhaps more to come, so everybody kind of waited. Hanging on. Finally Oolus asked, "Is . . . that it?"

Vent looked startled, as though coming out of a trance. "Of course."

Now everyone in the whole court looked a little puzzled at this point. The problem was that no one had really understood Vent's poem but nobody wanted to admit it (for fear they were the only one). So everyone smiled and waited to see what the King would do. But the King wasn't letting on.

"What think you, Illia?" he asked, looking blank. Illia stuck her tongue between her lips and blew a very loud rude sound known as a raspberry. Vent, who still seemed to be half in, half out of his poetic trance, looked very hurt at Illia's reaction, especially when everyone burst into laughter.

"Just as I thought, Vent . . . " the King said, a little embarrassed. "She, uh, loves it." Vent didn't quite know what to make of this. Nodding his head up and down and then back and forth he made his way back to stand with Ogo and Fub, who were both looking at him a little oddly.

"How about you, Ogo?" Oolus asked.

"Yes," said the King, "a poem about a rock. I don't know how that got in the toy box, but there you go. What have you got?"

"Sire," Ogo began humbly and courteously, "I confess my words are a little rough hewn as yet, but I hope to make up for that malady with melody."

"You're going to sing?"

"With your permission."

"By all means."

"A little rock song, shall we?" Oolus quipped. It wasn't really funny, but Oolus pulled her famed elastic face and for a second resembled Vent. Everyone laughed.

Holding the rock before him in both hands as though it were some holy relic, Ogo looked right at Princess Illia and in a rich and tuneful voice began to sing.

There is a rock —
A rock that holds the ocean.
There is a rock —
A rock that holds the land.
There is a rock —
A simple swaying motion —
This motion I am making with my hand.

50

Having half-walked, half-danced right up to the Princess Illia, Ogo now began to rock the rock back and forth in his arms as though it were a baby.

This is the rock, this is the rock,
The rock of east and west.
This is the rock, the almighty rock,
The rock that little babies love the best.

Across the room Vent shook his head disapprovingly, but nobody was confused this time — in fact, when Ogo finished his song the whole court except for Vent and Fub broke into instantaneous applause and Illia in a higher voice than anyone had thought possible squealed, "Gow! Gow!" The King, too, was obviously impressed. "Most inventive," he burbled.

"Well, Fub," said Oolus, when the applause had died down, "you've got a hard act to follow."

But Fub had been thinking fast and he was feeling wildly confident. Ignoring Oolus he turned and spoke to the King.

"Sire. I know what kids like these days. Sire, this poem is entitled 'The Lamb' and as you will see it actually invites the child to interact."

Fub began by stomping his right foot and swaying his body in a dance step which was right then very popular amongst the young men at court.

Once there was a lamb.
His mother's name was Ma'am, Ma'am the lamb.
But this lamb's name was Baa-aaa-am —
Baaam the lamb,

51

The mightiest lamb,
The bashingest lamb,
The lambastingest lamb in the land.
Baaaaam the conquering lamb.

All the time as he recited, Fub was swinging the lamb in a most violent fashion, punching and poking at the air in a way that was causing Illia to wince and hide her eyes. She peeked through her fingers as he stomped and Baaaaamed and shouted.

Oh Baaaaam was fierce,
He freaked the mice
And made the lions crawl.
He took the rattle
And went into battle
To smash that beast —

Fub looked around for some suitable opponent for the lamb. Something that rhymed.

— the Doll!

He screamed triumphantly. And with that he began to beat Illia's favourite toy over the head with the rattle, shouting,

O Baaaam! Baaaaam! Baaaaaam the lamb.

This did not go on very long. In a voice startling from one so small, Illia began to scream and squirm about in her father's arms, trying to rescue her doll. Apparently ignorant of the effect this was having on her, Fub just continued bashing until the King shouted, "Hey stop that! That's her favourite doll, you idiot." Fub stopped, astonished. "There, there," cooed the King to Illia, who was still kicking and shouting in a frenzy. Fub, seeing that she was upset, attempted to calm her by sticking his tongue out.

"Hey!" The King actually shouted. "I don't know what's worse, Fub," he said finally when the doll had been rescued and returned to Illia's loving and sobbing arms, "your judgement or your poetry. If my daughter were running this kingdom you would be in deep sh —"

"Shame," Oolus cut in.

"Thank you. Yes. Shame on you," the King said angrily to Fub. "You may be fierce in play fights, young man, but knighthood is also brotherhood and I fear your staggering lack of sensitivity. Still, you have not actually broken any rules. I must therefore allow your application for knighthood to go forward. Now go and stand with the others while I make my determination."

10
Three Quests

Incredibly, Fub had not yet grasped the serious-
ness of his mistake, for when he got over to Ogo
and Vent he whispered out of the side of his mouth,
"This is it! I can see he's impressed with me. I mean,
he has to act disapproving, but he likes me. I'm sure
of it."

Vent, whose face was almost pure white with
shock, answered, "He's an excellent actor then."

"You wait and see," Fub went on. "I will get the
best quest."

"Well, luck to both of you." Ogo held out his
hand. "As he said — knighthood is brotherhood."
Ogo shook hands with Vent but when he offered his
hand to Fub, Fub just swatted it away.

"Your attention, please!" Oolus interrupted. "After
much difficult deliberation His Majesty has finished
his assessment of these three worthy young men. As

you know there are three quests or tasks at this time. These tasks have been rated in order of difficulty and the most demanding task will be given to the most gifted of the young men. Your Majesty."

"Thank you, Oolus," the King said. "And so now — drum roll, please! The first applicant I will call upon is . . . Cornelius Hoophus —" Fub, who had been kneeling, literally shot up joyously and began to leap unceremoniously about the court as the boys in the crowd cheered. "I knew it! I knew it!" he cried. "Number one!"

Oolus allowed him to calm down and then said, "Congratulations, Fub, you are the very first . . ." Oolus paused ". . . to be assigned a quest today. A big hand for our second runner-up."

"Second runner-up. But . . ." Fub was astonished. The boys were aghast.

"It is a high honour indeed," the King smiled warningly at him.

"But Sire . . ." And here Fub fell into his most imploring and obsequious posture. "It has been my ambition since I was a child to lay the map at your feet, Sire — rim to rim — a cloak of countries spread for wisdom to walk over. I . . . I . . . I . . ." Fub's voice cracked and swelled with emotion.

"A moment, Your Majoosty." Oolus beckoned the King with a most mischievous look upon her face. While Fub continued to sputter she whispered in the King's ear something that caused him to laugh out loud.

"Oh that's a good one! Fub," he said, attempting to be serious now, "you have the mien of a man much concerned with matters of might."

"Most certainly, Sire."

"And would you be happy if I were to send you out against the Might of Awdor?"

"Oh yes, Sire. Yes, Sire."

"I thought you . . . might," said Oolus, and this poor pun caused not only Oolus and the King but the whole court, even Fub, to break up laughing.

"I do love it when you play with words, Oolus," the King said. Then, turning to Fub, who was looking much happier: "So you accept then?"

"Yes, Sire, yes, Sire," said Fub, falling at the King's feet and kind of squirming around in gratitude. "Oh thank you, blessed King."

"Yes, yes," the King said impatiently, gesturing Fub away with his hand. "Go."

"Don't be fooled by that runner-up stuff, kids," Fub whispered when he joined the others. "He's just being true to his blood. This is the real plum mission. Trust me."

Illia, however, was still feeling very upset about the treatment of her doll. She raised her arm and, pointing straight at Fub, called out. "Ma-agogglluuuguge!"

"Watch out!" Oolus screamed. "Grab his head fast!" Instantly two burly attendants darted across the floor, grabbed Fub's astonished head and held it fast in a double headlock, immovable. A look of great satisfaction entered Illia's eyes as Oolus thumbed quickly through her dictionary of magic terms.

Aiding her, the scribes spelled out loud, "M-a-dash-a-g-o-g-g — l-u-u-u-"

"A triple U?" Oolus asked. The scribes quickly compared notes.

"Triple U," they agreed.

"Okay then, let him go." The two men released Fub's head.

"You are very lucky, young man," Oolus said to Fub. "One syllable more and your head would have been . . ." Oolus emphasized her meaning by rotating her middle finger rapidly in the air, ". . . spinning." The whole court heard Fub gulp. His face turned very white and for a while at least he was very quiet.

"And now I call upon a very fortunate young man," the King said with a flourish. "Our first runner-up. Vent Pomandler."

Vent crossed the room to a smattering of applause.

"And where are you from, Vent?" the King asked.

"I have lived in many places, Sire. My father was in the army and we moved as the campaigns moved."

"And now you would move as a knight moves. Dark over land."

"Dark over land," Vent repeated.

"Swift over sand."

"Swift over sand," Vent repeated emotionally.

"Away! Away!"

Slapping the sides of their hips and doing a kind of stationary gallop, they both sang the refrain of the old empire song.

"Knights of the Endless Day."

"You know the song well, Vent," the King approved. "Yet I sense you are an unopened gift. Yes, yes, there is a knight within you, but it still lies wrapped in the chrysalis of dreaming. Go forth in fear, Vent, and take from the Wasteland of El-Oom the Great Garlic of Antibes, and carry it on to Orriador where you'll find this baby's mother, Queen Blue."

"Oh thank you, thank you, Sire. It's just what I wanted to do."

"And now for the most important quest of all, I call upon . . ." the King held up his hand for a drum roll ". . . Ogo McJones."

Solemnly Ogo crossed the court and stood before the King and Illia.

"Ogo, you are the finest broadswordsman, the fastest runner, the strongest swimmer, the best mathematician, a fine tactician and you even excel at the great art of blacksmithing. Now all of this is very good but you possess one quality above all that qualifies you for this very special mission. We have noted that you are an extremely kind young man."

"Yes, Sire."

"Therefore, Ogo McJones, I entrust the Royal Princess Illia to your keeping. Convey her to the land of Orriador where her mother Queen Blue is preparing her first birthday celebrations. This, Ogo, is your mission." There followed a loud drum roll which ended rather sooner than Fub had expected so that the whole court, including Illia, heard his loud and contemptuous whisper: "A babysitter!"

Suddenly terrified, Fub grabbed his head tightly in his two hands, but Illia only glowered and said nothing. The King also glowered at Fub and then continued speaking to Ogo.

"I was planning to take her myself, but now a war is threatened by the terrible Gannucks and I must go and talk to these bland people. But I made a promise to this baby's mother and I intend to keep it. Therefore, Ogo McJones, I entrust this baby's keeping to you."

Ogo didn't know whether to be happy or sad. "Why, Sire, I am truly honoured that you have chosen me for such a . . . a . . . dangerous task."

"Well, actually," the King smiled, "though this work is difficult, it is not really all that dangerous."

"Not dangerous?"

"No. I have no wish to endanger my daughter. And I must caution you against any kind of glory-seeking whatsoever. You will be taking the long, safe, northern route along the Blue Avenue to Orriador."

"But . . . shall I take my thrice-tempered titanium sword, Sire, in case we should meet, uh, a laughing giant there?"

"O yes, well, you should always take your sword with you," the King answered wisely, "but you are not likely to meet any laughing giants there."

"And shall I take my bow in case we're attacked by dragons?"

"You are not too likely to see any dragons there," advised the King, "except maybe way, way high in the sky where arrows won't go."

"No giants. No dragons." The court laughed.

"There is just one problem," Ogo dared to say.

Immediately the king's jocular manner changed and he spoke severely to Ogo. "Yes!"

"Sire, I have no horse . . . as yet."

"No horse!"

"None, Sire."

The King beckoned to Oolus and the two conferred privately.

"Not a problem. Not a problem, Ogo — no horse is necessary. You see, Illia tends to get horse-sick on long rides, so mostly I'm afraid you'll be walking her, or carrying her." Across the room Fub did his best to contain a rather malicious chortle.

Now something happened which Ogo would always remember. The King held out Illia so that Ogo might take her in his arms. Daintily and quickly Ogo removed his gauntlets, dropped them to the floor and reached for her. And what a feeling of wonder entered him as he held her for the first time! Right up close there was great magic in this baby's face. Her eyes were green as deep jade and her skin dark brown and smooth. Despite himself Ogo brimmed over into the biggest smile anyone had ever seen. Illia quietly returned his smile, nestling and burrowing into his strong, gentle arms.

"Just look how she is taking to you, Ogo," the King said a little enviously.

"Horg," Illia pronounced, looking calmly and trustingly right into Ogo's eyes, and Ogo began quietly to rock her back and forth. In seconds her head fell back and much to Fub's relief she fell asleep.

"Everyone," the King said happily, for he knew he had made a good choice in Ogo, "a big *quiet* cheer for Ogo." In a whisper all at court said, "Hooray!" and following the King and Oolus, they all marched off quietly singing that old song.

61

Dark over land,
Swift over sand,
Away! Away!
Knights of the Endless Day!

11

Hammer!
Hammer!

You must be very gentle with babies," said Wilming Twillingate, the King's top child-care expert. A very old, slightly hairy woman with a raspy voice, she was giving Ogo a quick tutorial in the task before him. "They are much more sensitive than adults and need a lot of swaddling and cuddling."

Ogo listened with a very eager look upon his face, taking in each detail fully, but inside he was confused. He was trying to figure out if he should be truly overjoyed or deeply disappointed at his quest.

"Illia has many magical texts that have been made for her by the genies and magicians of the known world and she loves to hear them, so you will have to become expert in a catalogue of slightly spurious animal sounds," Wilming lectured. "For instance, Oink, Moo, Hiss —"

"Yes yes, I think I know a lot of them already," Ogo cut in. Ogo was a good reader.

"Good. Good. And one other thing: Do not expect obedience from the Princess. In my opinion there is far too much obedience everywhere these days. Obedience is ruining the world. No child should learn obedience just for the sake of obedience — but especially Illia, who will one day be queen of two realms. You must be patient with her and use persuasion. If something must be done, you must convince her, not force her. Except in the case of emergency — safety first, of course."

"Of course."

"You have already noticed that she has a very loud voice when she likes."

"Yes."

"Nothing to be done about that. She takes a lot of energy. But if you are open to it, she gives a lot back too. And I must tell you that she sometimes stays up very late, but then when she sleeps, she sleeps long and deep."

Afterwards Ogo found himself an old bent tree just right for sitting, and solemnly in the setting sunlight he sat there thinking on his task. He was still trying to find out what he thought about his quest. This was hard because it was difficult not to think about what all the other young men were obviously thinking about it. They were thinking it was silly. Some of them even thought it was a joke that the King was playing on this foolish commoner.

To and fro the feelings moved through Ogo as he sat there, swinging his legs — anger, resentment, regret. Slowly he felt his way through them. He thought of Illia, of her Moxie green eyes that really did tickle something very deep and jolly in him. He thought of her picture books and rattles and bonnets and then he thought of the armour he had made for himself. He pictured the weapons he had made for the slaying of giants, for the conquering of dragons and the subduing of wild physical things and slowly, clarity, certainty, entered him. He knew what he had to do.

While the other men went about the solitary tasks of their own vigils, Ogo sought a special place in the King's compound, a place whose workings he was very familiar with. There was a cold, hard look in his face. He stoked up a fire in the kiln till the coals were super-hot and the forge began to glow. Then, quietly, as is the way of his people, he prepared to pray.

"O Hephaestus, God of the Smithy, such hard work I put into this breastplate. Such toil and hope. All that training so that I might be fierce and invulnerable — and now this. I am thwarted by my own kindness and tenderness. No dragons. No laughing giants. Just b-babysitting."

Ogo began to undo the clasps to his breastplate. "Well. Come," he said firmly. "I accept. As my dreams are undone so must this armour be undone. Come, fire. Come, hammer. Channel this rage . . ."

With that Ogo removed his breastplate. First he kissed it, then he placed it face down on the super-heated anvil. Taking the smith's heaviest hammer he began to pound at the breastplate, his face transformed in the glow — a series of hard diamond slabs. Cool fury and beauty. Rage and . . . As he hammered Ogo sang his smithy song.

Hammer, hammer,
Steel and coal,
Shape this steel
And the steel in my soul,
This steel in my soul,
This strength of man,
The song of the iron
And the iron in my hand.

No one could have helped but feel a sense of awe at the power and music in Ogo's voice.

Hammer, hammer,
You make me stammer,
This flash on flash
Of the heart.
Oh beat the earth
Or smash the pearl,
But change your shape
And we change the world.

The night, which had already been brooding and thick with humidity and the moon-worries of the people, now snapped open its big black bag of thunder and rain and began to hurl down its crackling energies upon the town and country all about. Ogo's singing and hammering stopped with the first crack of thunder and he ran to the window. "Ho blow, blow, you chill winds!" he called out. Then he flung open the two wide doors of the smithy so that the wild wind blew in, rushing through his hair and over his hammer and the coals, so that, stoked up, they burned ever more fiercely, releasing their long-held heat into the metal of the forge and the air about. And more the wind blew as he hammered, so strong that all was swept before it, and Ogo's hair flew back from him and his tunic blew back and the coals seared and spat with heat, white-hot in the big rush as he hammered and hammered.

"Surrender to my hammer's reason." Sparks flew as Ogo chanted. "Change your shape. Change your shape."

Suddenly, there was a calm in the storm as Ogo took up his song again.

Hammer, hammer, hammer,
Without you I am still a man,
But hammer, hammer, hammer,
you will always need my hand.
So hammer, hammer, hammer,
Change this steely shape.
Hammer, we change each other,
No matter what we make.

Finally, as the storm finished, Ogo's task was finished. He held up his handiwork and turned it round before his careful gaze. The breastplate was forever changed now. Satisfied with what he had done, Ogo walked off into the night.

12

The Parting

The King had ordered the entire court to assemble in order to see the young men off on their quests. And there they all stood with their pennants waving — ladies-in-waiting, men-at-arms, pages, chancellors, astrologers, advisors and petitioners, men, women, children, Fub, Vent, Oolu . . . Everybody but —

"Where's Ogo?" the King asked, a little irritably.

"Oh, he'll be along any moment now, Your Majesty," Oolus replied. "The young fellow has just been learning a few necessary, uh, child-care techniques and — well, Sire, he showed us a rather novel new way of tying a knot in a diaper."

"Yes. He's a brilliant fellow," said the King.

"All rise! The Princess Illia!"

There was something not quite right about Ogo when he finally appeared. His great cloak was drawn about him but beneath it there was a large swelling as though he had grown stout about the chest and belly. Not only that, but hanging from his staff was a bag of what appeared to be diapers. No one quite knew whether to laugh or not. But when Ogo bowed and a doll fell to the ground from a knapsack which he had attached to his back, the problem was solved.

"O, brilliant Uggers!" Fub snorted, as everyone laughed.

"What on earth have you done to your armour?" the King asked.

"I have redesigned it for my quest, Sire." Ogo blushed as he drew back the cloak to reveal his newly designed breastplate. Where before it had fit neatly to his chest, flattening out over his stomach, there was now a round bubble shape giving Ogo the look of a fat man. On one side of this bubble there were hinges for a little door which Ogo deftly swung open.

"Peekaboo," he said — and there, nestled inside, comfortable and squealing with delight, sat little Princess Illia.

"Why, there you are, my little Bombachuck," the King burbled. "Why this is very clever and arduous of you, Ogo. Now you can keep her protected no matter what happens."

"And not just protection, Your Majesty," the nanny added. "You see, babies like to cuddle and this is just numsee-peeko for that. Isn't it, my little Tum-a-lum?"

Here Fub laughed out loud. "Babies like to *cuddle!*" he snorted. The King glared at him, silencing him immediately. "O most wise Ogo," he almost

69

sang. "I grow more and more impressed with you."
Again Ogo blushed and Illia cooed.

"Sire, it is time for them to go," Oolus gently
reminded the King. "Perhaps you could give them
their oaths and start with the directions."

"Thank you, Oolus," replied the King. "Young
men! Please kneel."

Solemnly Ogo, Fub and Vent went down on their
knees before the king. This was the moment Moxies
in disguise had crept into court to see. *Oaves!*

"As you are about to embark on your sacred
quests," the King said, "I must ask three oaths of
you. Are you ready?"

"Yes, Sire," they answered as one.

"Do you swear never to turn away from anyone
seeking aid?"

"I do!"

"And do you swear to always keep your eyes
keen so that you may know when there are dragons about you?"

"I do," they answered.

"And do you swear never to crawl before giants?"

"I do."

"Ma!" Illia interjected gleefully, causing Fub to
reach nervously for his head.

"That's right, my little Bombachuck." The King
gave his daughter a gentle kiss on the cheek. "Now
I must give you your directions. Each of you must
set out upon this road. As I'm sure you know, it is
an ancient road and leads on to the crossroads at
Worldcleft Mountain, where there are three ancient
tunnels. Now, Fub, come with me." The King took
Fub aside and spoke to him alone. "Well, Fub, I see

71

you are ready to go on your dangerous mission."

"Ready and eager, Your Majesty."

"Listen to me clearly then, Fub. The middle tunnel is the way that you must go. It will take you straight to the country of Awdor which is close to the country of Orriador where Princess Illia's mother — the good Queen Blue — is staying. When you have subdued the Might of Awdor you must present yourself in fealty to Queen Blue with some token of your victory and, of course, my compliments."

"Yes, Sire — the middle tunnel. Thank you. Thank you so much."

"And be careful on your way, Fub, for the lands in between are the stalking grounds of various trolls and wickees. If you leave them alone they will probably leave you alone, but if you aggravate them they can be very fierce and deadly dangerous."

"I fear no trolls or wickees, Your Majesty."

"Forewarned is forearmed."

"Yes, Sire." Fub touched one hand to his electric chainsword. Fub was truly forearmed. "And thank you for this second runner-up quest."

Fub winked at the King as though there were some secret between them.

"Off with you now," the King replied, annoyed.

Mounting his charger, Fub gave it a good solid flick of the whip so that it started off at a gallop. Then, reining it in, he turned back and in a loud voice full of emotion called out, "Long live the King."

"Yah Yah!" the king muttered with a dismissive wave of his hand. Illia too waved her hand and spat out the single syllable "Baaa!" in a very expressive way.

"Come, Vent," the King beckoned, shaking his head. "Now I will instruct you." And again the King took Vent aside and spoke to him privately.

"When you get to the crossroads you must take the tunnel to the left which leads to the Wasteland. Now I must warn you, Vent, that this is a most dangerous mission. Once you enter the Wasteland no magical forces may rescue you, for there is no magic there. Chances are that as soon as you emerge from the tunnel you will be attacked by either a fierce and enraged griffin or a pterodactyl or both and there's no turning back — you can only go forward. If you get past the griffin and the pterodactyl you must proceed through a grim forest full of captive djinns in disguise. On the other side of the forest you will find the fabulous Garlic of Antibes. If you get the garlic you will still face many dangers before you can get out of the Wasteland, for there are many dragons, demons, dust storms, wickees and trolls there. And remember, there is only one way out of the Wasteland and that is over the Bridge of Abognath. This bridge is often guarded by the Laughing Giant, whom I'm sure you've heard of. Now if you can cross over this bridge you will be in the land of Orriador where Queen Blue is now. Present yourself with the garlic to her and give her my compliments."

"So it's the tunnel to the left?" said Vent. His face had turned a little white at this description of the terrors awaiting him. "And watch out for g-griffins, pterodactyls, dragons, demons, dust storms, wickees and trolls."

"And laughing giants," added the King ominously.

"Right! W-well, thank you, Sire." Trying not to show how terrified he was feeling, Vent mounted his horse.

"One more thing, Vent."

"Yes, Sire." Vent turned back eagerly, hoping for some reprieve.

"The Laughing Giant is no joke. He is deadly dangerous. Be careful and may luck be with you."

A wave of fear washed through Vent but he managed to answer, "Always, Sire!" in a voice quivering with emotion. "Long live the King!"

Vent galloped off down the road and was soon out of sight.

"And now you, Ogo, in whom I put so much trust," the King said. "When you get to the crossroads you must take the tunnel on the right that leads to Co-Zee. Once through the tunnel you will be in a safe and pleasant land wherein live many tiny puppies and sweet bluejays and the only thing you'll have to contend with will be Moxie tricks, which I assure you are completely harmless. Please take your time along this way, making sure to stop frequently for my daughter's pleasure. You may see in the middle of one or two meadows strange white gateways that seem to lead nowhere. These are ancient Moxie portals. Do not enter them for any reason. Just keep straight on the Blue Avenue and you shall come at your leisure to the land of Orriador where the Good Queen Blue is. When you arrive, please present yourself and my daughter to Her Majesty and bid her from me a happy birthing day and sweet memories."

"Yes, Sire."

"And make sure that you talk to Illia a lot." A very melancholy tone had now entered the King's voice. Everyone present felt his sadness.

"Yes, Sire," Ogo replied solemnly.

"Come, I will walk you as far as the bridge."

And so off they went, Ogo and Illia, the King, Oolus, nanny, chancellors and astrologers, peasants and guildsmen, all in a line, all a little sad.

After a while the King took Illia from Ogo. "Here, I will carry her awhile," he said quietly. The King hated saying goodbye but his duty called him and this is one of the hardest things about being a King. Drawing near the bridge he sang an old song that his mother had sung to him when he was a baby.

So long my little child,
I'll be with you in the wild.
Though winds shall howl and trees shall bend,
Be unafraid for all storms end.
But never, love, this is not parting,
Together forever, my little one,
My little lavender blue.

Gently the King gave Illia a kiss and handed her back to Ogo, but Illia too was feeling sad. She turned in Ogo's arms, reached back and gave her father one last hug.

"Da! Da!" she called out.

"She said Da!" The King smiled and kissed her gently on the cheek. "Have a happy birthday, my little one," he said. And now they parted.

Slowly Ogo walked away while Illia looked back,

waving and smiling. As one the whole court waved back and wept. Then Ogo turned and saluted.

"Long live His Majesty," he said gently.

The nanny, who was openly sobbing, called after him, "And remember — absolutely no sugar!"

13
The
Crossroads

In the centre of the crossroads stood what had once been a giant statue of an ancient Moxie prince. Once this statue had pointed the way for travellers, but that was long ago. Nothing now remained but a pedestal and the sculpted stump of one giant boot. Instead someone had erected a small signpost with arrows pointing to each of the three tunnels — El-Oom on the left, Awdor in the middle and Co-Zee on the right.

Standing before the tunnel to Awdor, Fub prayed to his god of war. He was just about to enter the dark tunnel when he heard a song in the distance, a song he had grown to enjoy foiling.

"Even bad luck turns to better . . ."

Fub could not resist. Quick and without a single jangle of chain, he hid behind the pedestal of the ancient statue and waited, the only noise the strangled sound of giggling in his throat. Finally a rather nervous looking Vent approached. Fub waited until Vent passed by the pedestal and then he attacked.

"Be bold or be bowled over," he yelled, giving Vent a good solid kick in the knee from behind so that he keeled over backward. Fub crowed like a cockerel, did some flash moves with his staff and was about to give Vent a hand up, when Vent came soaring up sword first and the two proceeded quite angrily to go at it. *Clang! Clang!* And in one flurry when both lost balance a little, there was a big backward lunging twirl that upended both of them and with a freak crack of the staff also struck the frail signpost so that it turned completely around, north to south. Unfortunately they were both so caught up in the battle that neither of them noticed.

Eventually Sir Fub the Conqueror, the Black Knight, did with full many blows smite a great *ker-plumpf* upon Vent's skull, thus conking him good and bringing him down. Fub, breathing heavily, still giggling, sprang to the gate into Awdor and with big shrieks of "Fub! Fub!" was out of sight and soon, as the mountain tunnel swallowed him up, out of sound.

Vent rose to his feet angrily. He felt like chasing Fub but alas he had this mission at hand. This terrifying mission. For you see, Vent was not really feeling as brave as he might like. This was the real thing. Now with his eyes slightly out of focus, a ringing in his ears and a reverberating in his bones, he was beginning to feel a bit unsure of himself. But Vent had learned to deal with this. He breathed in and breathed out deeply. Touching his lucky

78

medallion, he thought of calm river water slowly flowing while the bright sun shone in its reflection. Soon that shine was in his bones and Vent's confidence began to return. Finally calm, he examined the signpost.

"Wow, that blow must've really jangled me," he muttered to himself. "I could have sworn the King said the Wasteland was the tunnel to the left. Oh well, now I must go the most dangerous way I've ever gone. I can only pray that my faith and good luck will hold." And with that, noticeably trembling, Vent opened the gateway and cautiously disappeared into the tunnel.

Ogo and Illia were getting along wonderfully. Her delight in this newfound friend was just brimming over so that she beamed out radiant and dazzling smiles. And, of course, it brought out the best in Ogo to be so appreciated. Before he was even aware of it, he found himself putting on a show for Illia's applause. Every little funny face, every pulled down mouth and mock-crying eye seemed to tickle her funny bone till she was almost tired with laughter. And Ogo was so absorbed he was at best only half-aware of his surroundings.

"And what does the horse say?" he asked her. This was a sound that Illia had just learned. "Neigh!" she answered proudly as they neared the crossroads.

"That's right. Neigh. Aren't you a smart little girl? But tell me," he asked, "What does the horse say when the lion asks for a little ride?"

"Neigh!" Illia answered for the second time.

"Why, you're absolutely correct," Ogo said. "That's quite amazing. But I bet you don't know what the horse says when they ask it to pay taxes."

Again Illia knew the answer. "Neigh!"

"Well, riddle me — I can't believe it. You're just the smartest baby. I have just one more question for you. What does the horse say to the big question 'Is there anyone smarter than Ogo himself?' "

Just then, a wild black horse appeared before them. Ogo looked up and there it was, not ten feet away, staring back at him. Lifting its head almost as though in greeting, it answered "Neigh!" And it was so close, Ogo knew he could catch it. In fact, he was so overcome with this idea that for a moment he bent to the ground with Illia as though to put her there while he pursued. But before she touched down, he realized he couldn't leave her untended like that. Illia let out an angry cry. "Hey!" And then the horse was gone. It darted up some path in the mountains Ogo couldn't see. And Illia continued to cry.

"Oh no." Ogo stamped his foot in frustration, but this only made Illia cry more. "There, there," he soothed her. "Don't you worry. That horse is not so important. This was just a first meeting. One day we'll meet that horse again. It knows one day it will be mine. Don't you think so, Illia? Don't you think that horse will be mine?"

Cheering up, Illia answered as she always did. "Neigh," she said. And that, finally, was when Ogo turned to read the signs.

"But isn't that funny?" he said. "I could have sworn the King said that Co-Zee was the tunnel to the right! Hmmm. What tricks memory plays. Co-Zee it says — and points to the left. Well, I guess it depends which way you're facing. Good thing I can read. I might have taken the wrong way and wound up in the Wasteland! What a terrible thought."

Ogo gave Illia a big swooping swing back into the breastplate place and then, dancing playfully, opened the gate and entered the tunnel — the tunnel that only the crazed, the maddened, the glory-hungry or misinformed enter. But there was no ominous shriek, no gust of gloom to warn the two happy travellers. The ancient gate shut quietly behind them and swung softly to a standstill.

14

The Forest of Pleaders

As Ogo and Illia walked through the tunnel in the mountain, unknown to them, a great storm brewed over the Wasteland. The griffin who guarded the gate on the other side, pawed the ground eagerly, sensing something tasty coming through the tunnel. And the pterodactyl who watched the griffin watched ever more closely, waiting for its moment.

All around, the ground was littered with the broken bones of the griffin's last feast — a careless unicorn who had ventured too near the gate — but still the griffin was hungry and still the pterodactyl watched, wanting something soft and yielding in its mouth. Beside the river, a gnarled, imploring tree also watched, saying nothing.

When the rain began to fall the griffin ventured from its cave, hoping to hide beside the gate in ambush, for surely something was coming. That was when the pterodactyl dropped from its high peak, with deadly accuracy. Too late, the griffin looked up. The pterodactyl's claws were already upon it.

While Ogo trudged peacefully through the dark of the mountain a fierce fight ensued. And even as the fury of the beasts escalated, so did the powers of the storm. Claws ripped flesh, teeth bit into sinew, great howls of pain and rage contested with the deep thunder and patter of rain. The animals were equally matched and soon settled into a mutual death embrace, each one holding the other fast — the griffin, clawing away with its bottom legs at the pterodactyl's belly, while the big sharp beak of the pterodactyl made a bloody ruin of the griffin's many eyes. Now as they struggled to a standstill, both of them losers, the rain pounded down about them, washing all over the steaming rocks and the littered, gouged terrain, sweeping all before it in a thousand tiny, swelling streams to the river that grew bigger and muddier and bloodier with their struggles.

Terrible shrieks of agony arose from the pterodactyl's beak as the griffin's claws found its entrails. In a final burst of strength it lifted its mighty wings one more time, serving only to turn the two of them over and over with the flapping and off into the gorged and bloody river. Cawing, shrieking, bellowing with rage, the two animals struggled in vain to free themselves, but no peace was possible now. The river dragged them away, rolling and turning, wider and deeper, until their struggles ceased and their cries subsided and they were swept away and drowned.

83

Still the rain pounded down upon the bare, rocky ground, washing all the blood and bones and feathers away while the gnarled tree clung to the bedrock.

As suddenly as they had started, the rain and thunder stopped. For a while, the mighty wind continued to blow, frothing up the contrary motions of the river, sweeping everything clean, so that for the first time in a long time the blue stone of an ancient road was visible. Then something rare happened — the sun came out. Its golden rays poured down upon the fresh-washed ground and for a little while, this place looked as it had in days of old when Moxie princes had roamed here, and cartloads of amber and jade had come glinting through the mountain tunnel on the way to Orriador and all the lands of the Endless Day. And that was when Ogo, with Illia deeply asleep inside his breastplate, emerged from the tunnel and unknowingly entered the Wasteland of El-Oom.

If he had arrived on a more typical day Ogo would have encountered gloom, a griffin and a pterodactyl and he would have known immediately that he had made a terrible mistake. Instead, he was met with glorious sunlight, a newly washed blue road, no pterodactyl, no griffin and there, as chance would have it, a bluejay flew by. Still, the landscape was bare and craggy and steaming. And over by the riverside a rather ominous looking tree almost seemed to walk for a moment.

"This is Co-Zee?" Ogo asked aloud. "Not quite how I pictured it. Not exactly a pleasure garden, actually. Something not quite right here. I can smell

84

it in the air." Indeed there was a strange odour about the place. "Something sinister. Something dreadful. Its almost as though some beast had . . ." Ogo checked his feet to see if he had perhaps stepped in some animal spoor. "Nope." He walked away but the stink went with him. In fact it seemed to be following him around. "Where is it?" Why, it seemed to be right . . . under . . . his . . . nose. Just then Illia awoke inside Ogo's armour and let out a cry, and Ogo realized what that smell was.

"Oh! Oh! I see," he said with a laugh. "Oh well, it's time for you to come out of there anyway." Ogo placed his shield face down on the ground. "Well, let's do it," he said cheerfully.

Ogo placed Illia comfortably on the shield, took a clean diaper from his pack and gently and respectfully went about his task. As he worked he sang in a jolly voice.

I thought I'd be a mighty knight,
My might in thought and deed,
My sword an iron lightning bolt,
The thunder for a steed.
I thought I'd fight in dragons' lairs
All tangled up in vipers,
I could've changed the way things are,
But now — I'm changing diapers.

And hail the rose, the rose, the rose,
And the holly, holly green,
Oh salute you perfumed lilac buds
And your stems of gabardine,
Oh praise your long parade of blooms,

Oh play, you perfumed pipers,
I could've bathed in sweet perfumes,
But now — I'm changing diapers.

What use this magic sword of mine,
The child rocks in my shield,
As though there were no quests to take,
No beast or battlefield.
Now are all my arms reduced
To pins and bibs and wipers,
These mighty hands that swung the sword —
Aaah now — they're changing diapers.

Having removed the dirty diaper Ogo took Illia
over to the river, which was much calmer now, and
bathed her bottom in it. Illia loved the cool water
and for a while she kicked and splashed in it. But
she was still sleepy, her eyes cloudy with
undreamed dreams. Deftly Ogo put on her clean
diaper, singing more quietly now.

So hail the rose, the rose, the rose,
The holly, holly green,
Oh salute, you perfumed lilac buds
With your stems of gabardine,
O praise to moons and babies' bums
And fie all whine and gripers.
She needs some fresh air . . . everywhere,
And so — I'm changing diapers.
One day I'll change the way things are,
Today I've changed her diapers.

By the time he had finished the song Illia was

asleep. Lifting her lovingly into the breastplate place, Ogo repacked the bags, took two steps on the Blue Avenue and . . . there . . . that tree seemed to move again. Yes. It was definitely coming toward him. Quickly Ogo drew his sword. Was this some Moxie trick? In a terrible, deep, swamp-like voice the tree moaned.

"oooooh. The nuts. The nuts. They're driving me nuts. Oh prithee. Please, Sir Knight, can you not help me? I have nuts in my head." The tree shook its head, causing something inside to rattle. "Can you not strike, Sire — right here — and get them out? Oh please! Please!" Ogo raised his sword, uncertainly moving closer.

Just then a giant stone cried out in a great cracking voice, "Please! Please! The river is carrying off our pearls! It's stealing the fish from the lakes and carrying them down to the all-drowning sea. Can you not strike with your metal the heart of this river, Sire?" But before Ogo could strike, other voices arose — stones, flowers, leaves all seemed to cry out. "Please! Please! Please! Free us!" The agony in these voices was terrible and Ogo had not forgotten his oath to the King. But he was also remembering his oath to his mother.

"Oh alas, alas," he called out, "I feel deeply your terrible agony, but I cannot help you."

"What? Did you not swear to your King to give aid, Sir Knight?" the tree bellowed, and it began to follow him.

"Oh alas, alas, I did, brother oaken-mouth," Ogo replied sorrowfully, "but I have also sworn to my very mother never to raise this sword against the

87

earth, and a tree is of the earth, as the soil and stones and rivers are of the earth."

"Oath breaker!" the tree shrieked desperately, and it seemed almost as though it might attack Ogo.

"No!" Ogo shouted quite loudly.

This set them all off again, wailing and beseeching. "PLEASE! PLEASE! HELP ME! PLEASE!" But by now Ogo knew there was something amiss. Perhaps this was some kind of Moxie mischief.

"I'm sorry but I can't help you," he shouted again over the din.

"Accursed coward," the tree bellowed at him in its deep-rooted voice. "Promise breaker! You shall pay for this. You shall pay! Oh Please! Please! Help me!"

It was very hard for Ogo to do, for he had sworn an oath never to turn away from cries for help, but he turned his back then and walked away from all the stones and trees and roots as they cursed and pleaded with him. And the farther he walked the more importuning were their wailings, so that it tugged at his very heart to continue.

"Please! Oh prithee!" the grass whined in its myriad voice — "Slay this soil that imprisons us." "Oh I beseech thee," leaves cried out. "Oh cut out the evil heartwood of this tree that holds us here fastened in its greedy grip." Still Ogo continued on his way through the immense forest. "O succor, succor!" cried the rocks. "Beat this earth that has frozen us and cast us out — we who once ran in molten merriment. We who were once star stuff. Bid it open and receive us once again. Cut! Cut! Cut!" But now Ogo was running. His feet were fast as he kept to the blue road, but his heart was sore within him at the vow of service he was breaking. "I am cursed!" he thought to himself. "Either I break one sacred vow or I break another."

After what seemed like hours the pleading forest fell away from the road and a most sweet and penetrating aroma began to waft into Ogo's nostrils. Soon he came to a gate in a high brick wall and found himself in a well-tended garden wherein many elegant purple flowers bobbed atop green stems higher than Ogo's head. What was that aroma? It was making him salivate and tingle and breathe deeply but he couldn't quite place it.

Suddenly a tall and elegant woman or spirit in a green and purple gown appeared before Ogo.

"Hail, Sir Knight." Her voice was warm and inviting. "Well done. You have come through the Forest of Pleaders."

"The Forest of Pleaders?"

"Yes," the woman continued, tall and swaying and magnetic. "Didn't you know? Were you not approached by my many pleading creatures with absurd crises?"

"Yes," Ogo confessed sadly, "but I could not help them."

"Oh, but that is a good thing," the woman said. "You have come through a great trial. For these were not true trees and plants in distress. These are captive djinns who have been imprisoned here for excessive violence. If you had struck as they requested they would have been released from their prison. They would have been free to attack and subdue you."

89

"Well, thank the Goddess for the oath my mother made me make!" Ogo said, relieved. "I knew there was something strange about that place." Later Ogo would wish he had stopped a while and asked a few more questions, but right now he was fascinated by this magical being who stood before him. "But who are you?" he asked.

"I am the Goleen of Garlic." The elegant woman sighed and swayed and Ogo sighed and swayed with her, a great sense of relaxation and relief washing through him.

"You are the first one to come through in many a long moon," she cooed and swayed. "And to you goes the Great Garlic of Antibes. Enough to feed all — a great pesto of the tribes."

"But I am not bid retrieve the fabulous Garlic of Antibes and my mother made me swear never to raise my sword against the earth."

"No, the time is right," she persisted gently, hypnotically. "You must take it. Harvest at the right time is not violence."

Ogo's senses were swimming in a sea of garlic and perhaps he wasn't thinking clearly. "Well, maybe I can somehow get it to Vent," he said dreamily.

At her instruction, and still magnetized by her green gaze, Ogo took out his sword and dug into the earth in a place she indicated. Soon he uncovered a many-cloved giant bulb that was so aromatic, so sweet and enticing, he could not help but swallow ceaselessly to smell it. Bending low he lifted from its place in the soil a great garlic the size of a boulder.

"Mmmmmm. It smells so good!" he sighed. "But how am I going to carry it? I know — I shall use the snuggly!" Still staring into the Goleen's magnificent eyes, Ogo stuffed the huge garlic into the snuggly which Illia's nanny had given him and managed to sling it over his back.

"Good! Good!" the Goleen cooed. And she too took a good hearty sniff at the garlic.

"I must go now," Ogo said, "for I am bound for..."

"Adieu, adieu, sweet knight," the Goleen interrupted him. She hated to be the last to say good-bye. "Off you go now. Adieu. Adieu." She kissed him on the cheek. Ogo's senses tingled in a kind of ecstasy at the closeness of her warmth and scent.

"Adieu, adieu to you too." He sighed and began to walk away with the garlic on his back. Soon he came to the gate in the great wall which enclosed the garden. Here he turned to say "Adieu" one more time, but the Goleen was gone. Ogo passed through the gate to a place of slowly rising hills, and was soon on his way. "How must Vent and Fub be doing?" he wondered as Illia, deep in a dream of garlic, turned over in his breastplate. "I mean, if this has been a pleasant little stroll, those poor fellows must be in truly terrible circumstances."

Ogo had hardly been gone a few minutes when the Goleen came running back to the gate, with a worried look upon her face.

"Oh I forgot," she called out after him. "Dragons! Dragons have been sighted!" But it was too late. Ogo was out of earshot and she must stay here inside the garden forever. "Be wary, good Sire!" she called out. "O dear Kali, protect him. He has gone, gone, gone."

15

Toxic Troll

Fub had made good time. With great speed he had trekked through the tunnel and now galloped full speed along the road to Awdor. He'd been down old Moxie lanes before and had come to despise them for their smallness, so narrow his big broad sure-footed steed was hard pressed to keep from stepping over the edge as he drove it mercilessly onward, never stopping.

Slowly the landscape began to change around him. The forest which at the beginning of the road had been tall and dense began to thin out. Occasionally he began to note with approval the appearance of stumps where attempts had been made to clear the land. Soon there were more and more clearings and fewer and fewer trees. And less and less of that wild racket of birds that he half-hated and half-loved. Eager for battle he spurred his huge horse onward deep into the country of the Paper People where the land was tilled and contoured with the marks of ploughs.

As he galloped, Fub day-dreamed about his upcoming battle. All he knew about Awdor was that it was a swampy region. What the people who lived there were like he did not know, but such was his confidence in his own prowess he never once doubted he could conquer them single-handedly.

After all he was superbly trained, supremely psyched and — here he touched the brim of his cannon hat, and the hilt of his chainsword — extremely well equipped.

Not till late in the afternoon did the gloating Fub allow his poor thirsty horse to take rest and water. Ahead the narrow road followed the river for about another quarter of a mile. Then, abruptly, there was one of those ancient Moxie portals and beside it, a bridge. Under the bridge Fub saw something that thrilled him — a very hungry looking troll. Fub had many delights in life, but few could equal his pleasure in tormenting trolls. "Ha!" Fub rubbed his hands gleefully together and, retrieving his horse, proceeded to lead it quietly and covertly toward the bridge.

"Oh hungry! Hungry I!" the troll kept muttering as he scratched his raw, green skin and stank. It had been a long time since anything weak and tasty had ventured this way, and the troll was getting very hungry. And the more he hungered the more he itched and the more he itched the more he scratched and stank so that he was very raw and very stinking indeed, even by troll standards. He felt like giving up and going home, but the thought of taking slugs home to his family for dinner yet again was too daunting. Raking his claws obsessively over his flesh, the troll watched and waited and hoped.

Just then, to his surprise there was the sound of a footstep on the bridge. What! Lizard-quick the troll hissed to his feet and peered up over the railing. There he spied what actually looked like . . . a man. A man! A man! A big man and very well armoured, but the troll was bigger and hungrier. With a mighty thrust of his big lizard legs the troll sprang up right in front of the unwary traveller.

"Eek! A troll!" the man cried out and fell down gasping, one hand over his heart. Six steel daggers, the troll's claws sprang open for the kill and his upper lip lifted, revealing two long, curved fangs. Weakly Fub begged, "Oh no, Mr. Troll, please don't eat me. I'm far too tough."

The troll was not listening. He was hungry and itchy. He stretched out his claws and licked his lips. "Mmmmmmm. Hungry, hungry I!" So Fub begged some more. "Oh please, Mr. Troll, I am far too bony and tough. You'd much prefer my elder brother."

The troll had not heard this one before. "Why?"

"He's so much more tender and fleshy than me." Fub's voice had diminished to not much more than a squeak. "And besides — he doesn't have one of THESE!" Shouting this final word, Fub gave a quick yank on the cord of the electric chainsword and its high unnerving *Buzzzzzz!* cut through the air.

Snake-like the troll cringed back. He bared his terrible fangs and made ready to spit his green

94

poison at Fub, but Fub just touched him on the shoulder with his buzzing blade and there was a great screech as scales flew off and green blood bled. The troll cried out "No!" in a voice that was terrible to hear, deep and gutteral, full of misery, injustice and bitterness. "No, no," he kept whining in terror, backing away from the terrible buzzing blade. But Fub just laughed out loud and kept swinging at him until he ran away crying, and hid in the rocks and the ruin.

"Well, hail swordsmanship," Fub scoffed, turning off the chainsword. From far away, seething with humiliation, the toxic troll scratched in fury and watched helplessly as Fub mounted his tired horse and rode off over the bridge out of sight. When he was sure Fub was out of the way the troll returned to his place beneath the bridge, and once more, with even more pain and more poison, he began to wait and watch.

"Big man wif chainsword yefff." the troll hissed through his fangs. "Yeffff, he ivvv. Very big. Bigger than hungry I. And a *funny* man too." This made the troll so angry he beat his fist into his palm and jumped and gargled from deep within his froggy throat. "How I hate him and all hivvv flaughtering and laughing kind." The troll punched his fist into his palm and jumped with each spat-out word. "How gladly I would take them on one on one without theve cheating weaponf of theirv. Well, I'll get the next one." And with that the troll squatted down under the bridge beside the Moxie portal and melted into the shadows, unseeable.

16
Terrors of Co-Zee

In the little light allowed by the wrought-iron gate at the end of the tunnel, Vent paused to catch his breath and calm once again his terrified nerves. Ever since he had first read about them in school he had suffered from a terrible condition known as "Fear of Griffins." All his life he had dreaded this awful moment when he must finally encounter one face to face, and now his skin crawled with the knowledge of the almost certain agony that awaited him. For a long time he just shivered there, almost ready to turn on his heel and abandon this quest. Fortunately, the warmth of his lucky talisman calmed his worried hand. And besides, the thought of shame terrified him even more than death. Drawing his shield about him, he gripped his sword as tight as possible, pushed the gate open with one foot and peered out into the green and sunny valley before him.

Vent was not fooled by the cheerful chirping of birds in the trees. Nor did the merry gurgle of the brook calm him or induce him in any way to let down his guard. With his back to whatever canyon wall or rock he could dart or crawl to, he proceeded terrified into . . . Co-Zee.

Cautiously he surveyed the sky. Sunlight. Deep endless blue skies. Distant mountaintops, crags, cliffs. And what about pterodactyls? Suddenly there was a yelp and something that might have been a very small griffin ran out of the trees and charged at Vent. Really it was one of the many puppies the King had told Ogo about, but Vent was too terrified to see this. He saw a little griffin lunging at him and he began to run pell mell, screaming as the puppy wagged its tail playfully and ran along behind. Vent didn't get very far before he tripped over a stone and crashed headlong into the ground. Right away the puppy was upon him. "No, no!" Vent screamed. But the puppy just kept leaping about trying to get at Vent's face. "No! Please! Do not baste me with your black and deathly breath!" Then Vent felt something warm and a little rough, a little ticklish on his cheek. The puppy was licking him. This was Vent's worst nightmare come true but he met the challenge masterfully. Full of an energy and power he never knew he had, he cast the puppy off with a mighty thrust of his arms, and then, standing tall, reached for his sword. But by then the battle was over — the terrible puppy tucked its tail between its legs and scampered away.

"O Lady Luck. O Diana." Trembling but victorious the mighty Vent fell upon his knees and gave thanks to the Goddess.

The blue road to Orriador now stretched before Vent and would have been easy enough to follow, but he was feeling powerful and lucky. For off to the side of the road, just up ahead, there was an ornate portal which seemed to lead nowhere. This was one of those Moxie portals which the King had advised Ogo about, but Vent didn't know that. He thought it must be a lucky short cut, as many such portals were. And his intuition was telling him, "Go . . . go forward."

"Well, so long, griffin," he said, dusting off his hands. "Lady Luck is with me yet. I have never doubted her." And with that he entered the portal.

17

Dangungs!

Ogo was very tired as he continued to climb the ever-rising Blue Avenue. He might have long ago had a feeling that something was very wrong with this journey but all his senses were saturated with the scent of garlic and for the past seventeen hours Illia had been wide awake — and demanding. For instance, she had insisted that they stop very often to examine the sights along the way. Every flower, every stone, even things invisible to Ogo caught her attention. And once she had noticed a thing, she wanted to touch it and coo over it or dance round it or ride Ogo galloping over it. Very often she wanted to sit quietly in front of it and just study it. Ogo complied with his most cheerful manner and dutifully galloped as often as demanded. Neighing upon command. Brinnying. Bucking. He even simulated the eating of grass quite cheerfully.

And so they proceeded sight by sight through the Wasteland of El-Oom, completely unaware of the dangers about them. Evening was coming on, and the road began to rise into distant foothills, and from there, high and higher, into a range of mountains, misty peaks and volcanoes. Towards these, with Illia shouting "Puh, puh" on his back, Ogo now climbed.

Not too far ahead of them there was an ancient and sacred place known as the Vale of Vharn. Here, as the sun sank, a blank and elegant silhouette of dragon wings slowly descended and landed, sniffing the ground and walking a while, circling, then curling up and — with a snort of relaxing smoke — going to sleep. Then another dragon landed and likewise went to sleep. Both dragons in the twilight looked like small hills — immovable boulders. Now another, smaller dragon touched down, and another, and another and another. The sky was full of them so that their wings almost entirely blotted out what was left of the sunlight. Soon a whole herd of dragons had landed, crept and searched and now slept, still as stone, as dragons always do.

By the time Ogo got to the Vale it was almost completely dark and he was very tired. The grass and flowers were still visible, though, for from afar, distant volcanoes cast another kind of light. From deep inside itself the earth's star stuff glowed and simmered with deep space magic. Normally Ogo would have noticed the distinctive aroma of dragons, but to him everything still smelled of garlic, garlic, garlic. All Ogo could see was that the grass was soft and that there were what he took to be high protective boulders all around. Deciding that this would be a good place to rest, he quietly set up camp.

Fortunately Illia too was by now getting drowsy. All day Ogo had been trying to teach her to say his name. "It's Ogo," he tried again. "O and Go. Ogo. Can you say it?" But Illia responded strangely. She made a sound from one of her animal books. She went "*Haaaaaw!*" and pointed into the night.

"That's very good," said Ogo tiredly. "But my name isn't *Haaaaaw!*"

Illia persisted. "*Haaaaaw!*" she said again.

"Yes. Well, it's quiet time now, Illia." Ogo continued to set up camp. "*Haaaaaaw!*" said Illia.

"See how dark it is," Ogo said patiently. "Quiet time."

"*Haaaaaaaw!*" Illia replied.

"Yes, you do a very good dragon, my little Flame, but it is quiet time now."

Just then one of the baby dragons who were sleeping all around them stirred in her sleep. She was having a dream about people and let out a little gust. "*Haaaaaaaaw!*" said the real dragon.

"Wow! That was really good," Ogo said, impressed, thinking it had been Illia. "Do you do prime ministers?"

But now Illia was pointing. "*Haaaw. Haaaaw. Dangungs.*"

"Oh, I see what you mean," replied Ogo sleepily. "Yes, it does look a bit like dragon fire, doesn't it? You're so imaginative. But really those are far-away volcanoes. Don't you remember your daddy told us about the volcanoes in Co-Zee?" All the

101

while as Ogo spoke he was gently rocking Illia in his arms.

Again Illia made her little dragon noise: "*Haaaaaw.*" But the rocking was having its effect and to help it along Ogo had begun to hum an old lullabye. Slowly, slowly, Illia's eyes closed.

Ogo was tired too. He placed the garlic on the ground beside him and securing Illia in his breast-plate he curled up on the grass. Soon he fell into a deep and sweet, garlic-saturated sleep. In fact so deeply did Ogo sleep that he didn't hear the windy flutter of yet another dragon in the sky above them, a giant dragon who carried in its flame a vision of its own face, high-fanged and cruel. This dragon landed softly, and, as it was completely dark now, quietly used its own fireburst to find its way to a comfortable resting place. And there in the deep dark of Vharn, in the desolate heart of El-Oom, right beside Ogo and Illia, it fell asleep.

18

The Sacking
of Vent

There were several places the Moxie gate might have led Vent to that day, for when they work, Moxie gates work on wishes, and in the olden days one had only to step inside and wish for any of a thousand locations all around the Lands of the Endless Day, to be instantly transported there. But those days were so long gone now nobody, not even Moxies, remembered them. Kings and empires, queens and ages had passed since then. In fire, hurricane, flood and fury, by sandstorm or earthquake, by topplers and tippers, by all the work and winds of time 996 of those gates had been destroyed, or completely eroded to nothingness. Of the four that remained, one led to the forest of Gh'iz — halfway up a mountain where El-Oom met Awdor and Orriador. One led to brave Atlantis, where wonders still never ceased, one led to the earth's super-heated core. And one . . . only one led to a little stone bridge that crossed a river on the road to Awdor, and somehow, perhaps because he was picturing calm water as he entered, it was to this portal that Vent was transported.

Despite his faith in his intuition Vent was playing it smart. Keeping one foot inside the gate he peered out in all directions, sniffing and listening carefully. All he saw was a quiet, peaceful little bridge beside a softly flowing river on a beautiful summer day.

"Just as I thought," he said to himself confidently. "Safe as a mother's arms and I'm getting closer to the Great Garlic. I can almost smell it."

With that Vent sauntered out of the portal, and as he trod upon the bridge his heels rang out with the kind of staccato click only a truly jaunty fellow can make.

"Ahaaaaa!" was all the troll said from under the bridge. But his voice, twisted by rage, by centuries of injustice to trolls, was deep and lionic and full of hatred. Vent dropped into a combat squat and looked around in horror but could not see where the sound had come from. With a great PLUMPFF! the hateful troll leapt on to the bridge, landing right dead set in front of Vent. "Ahaaaaaaaaa!" This was another scene right out of one of Vent's nightmares. "O Lady Diana, guide my —" But Vent didn't finish the thought. Nor did his trembling hand make it those few last inches to his blade, for the troll grabbed Vent's wrist and held it tight and cold.

"Pleaved to meet you, Miffter Man," the troll hissed through his dripping fangs, as his other

105

hand, powerful and huge, wrapped itself round Vent's neck. "And where iv your chainfword now?" the troll asked in that deep, hate-full voice. Vent could ony gargle in hapless terror, wriggling and choking in the troll's green grip. Leaning over, the troll sniffed him. Once. Twice. "Hummmmm. You fmell fo good. You know I kind of like you. In fact, I want you to meet my whole family. Yef, why don't you come home for dinner? Of courfe you will want to wear a dinner jacket." So saying the troll bagged Vent. That is, he whipped out a large sack and with one quick, skillful yank, tugged it completely over Vent's terrified body right down to his feet. With ease the screaming, kicking Vent was then yanked upside down and slung over the troll's back, the sack tied tight.

"Oh, Oh, Oh, lucky me," sang the troll, doing a little dance of glee. "I've got me a man, a man, a man." Then the troll made his own exit through the Moxie portal and was soon walking along a path not far from his home in the mountain forest of Gh'iz. As he danced along, spinning Vent to keep him dizzy, the troll had a very happy look on his face. His partner — Mf. Troll — wav gonna love thif!

It might have been a very unlucky end for Vent, but fortunately on his way through the forest, the troll spotted a sausage on the side of the road and stopped to eat it. Ummmm, what a day! What a big juicy greasy stinking filthy old sausage. Mmmmm. Mmmmm. And there's another one. *Gulp*! And another. Hey wow. Look at all these sausages.

And the troll proceeded from one sausage to another, at first just a little off the path. And then

106

Gulp! Gulp! a little farther. Until suddenly there were no more big greasy stinking filthy old sausages. The troll looked up and it was getting dark and he realized he'd come all the way up the mountain to the plateau. He took one more incautious step in the deep grass when there was a loud TWANG!

Suddenly the troll was snared in an ever-tightening net, yanked upside down and hung from a tree. Screaming, he kicked and clawed and bucked and squawked in rage, but he couldn't get free. And then he remembered that on his back in a sack he had a very tasty man. Vent trembled — a man in a sack on the back of a troll in a trap in a tree.

For a while the troll tried to get at Vent. But he was wrapped up too tight in the net and couldn't move very well. Vent, who was by now right side up, clung to the troll's upside-down back tightly, trying not to let the brutish creature get at him. When the troll finally realized he wasn't going to get at Vent, he started to plead.

"Come man. Help me. I'm forry. We're in thif togevver. I fouldn't have faid I'll eat you. You could get out of the fack and get uf both out. I promife I won't eat you." But Vent couldn't get out of the sack. He had tried already. So he said nothing and just clung on tight in the terrible stink, most of the night silently weeping and coughing. Poor Vent. Was this to be his good luck? Stuck all night nose down on a troll's back, in a sack in a trap in a tree?

19

Dragons Awake

On the other side of the Wasteland in Orriador, Queen Blue was thrilling at the idea of seeing her daughter again. As was her custom, she arose and beat her blue drum at the dawn of the day, singing as the Moxie children began to play. Gilded with endless dawn, her palace rose from a wilderness of meadows and ancient forests.

Dew was everywhere for all to drink. Dew that sparkled and made rainbows, dew on tall thistle rods, where ravens flew in multitudes and pelicans pawed at the earth for strawberries.

Unseen at first, there were Moxie dwellings melted into the landscape, absorbed in hills, hidden inside rocks, under hill-crest overhangs. Luminous, shifting. Dreamlike, magical. Many of the Moxies on this special day were busy gathering, in long thin-necked bottles, the glories of the dew.

108

Queen Blue sang with the Moxies as they gathered and joked, but despite herself she felt uneasy. Something, she felt, was not quite right.

Just then, in the Vale of Vharn, Ogo awoke with a start. That intoxicating scent of garlic still permeated the air and he breathed it in deeply. But there was another scent underneath the garlic scent. A scent he couldn't quite place. Ogo took another deep breath, stretched out his arms in a wide, luxurious yawn and touched something — something cold and scaly.

"Dragon!" The word screamed in Ogo's mind and he was on his feet in a second, his sword drawn and held before him. Seeing what had slept there, huge and green, beside him, Ogo gasped and gulped with disbelief. He had seen dragons from a distance before. Dragons the size of bears, dragons as large as pterodactyls. But this dragon could have cupped bears and elephants in one giant claw. Not even in fairy tales had he heard of anything so immense and fabulous and . . . beautiful as this. What a prize! What glory! Ogo raised his sword high, intending to thrust the blade deep into the dragon's sleeping neck but just as he did this Illia stirred within his breastplate and he hesitated, backing off a little. That was when he saw all the other dragons — big dragons, baby dragons, black, green and purple dragons, smouldering dragons and . . . there . . . one dragon who seemed to be stirring.

Again Ogo hesitated. He knew he could kill this one gigantic dragon, and all alone, with his speed, with his skill, perhaps he could avoid or evade the rest and live to drag that smouldering giant head back to His Majesty's feet. But he was not alone. He had a baby to look after. And now he remembered the King's warning about glory-seeking. No, he could not fight. Even though he had waited and trained all his life for this fight, he could not fight. Quietly, bitterly, his hand gripping his chain mail lest the smallest little tinkle of metal on metal awake one of these beasts, Ogo crept away from the dragons. And when he dared run, he ran as fast as he could. As fast as a coward might run.

Now the giant dragon opened its eyes in terror. It had been having a terrible dream of its own. A dream about that most terrible beast of all — man. *Sniff-sniff.* The dragon smelled garlic and . . .

"Children. Quick. Awake! Away!" It had not been a dream. A man had been here. "Oh away, away quickly — higher than arrows may fly."

Hiding behind a tree far down the other side of the height of Vharn, Ogo heard the thunderous flutter of many wings as the dragons rose from their resting place and flew away. He cursed to think of the glorious opportunity he had lost, and when the last of the dragons arose he cursed again, for tangled in its claws, still bound in Illia's snuggly, was the Great Garlic of Antibes.

20

Toxies

Look, we've got one!" a huge and terrible voice hollered. Excitedly, a creature whose body was as small as its voice was large stepped from a leaf shadow as the moon went down and pointed to the trap in which Vent and the troll were hanging. A multitude of other big voices responded with shrieks and screams and several other small creatures appeared. Inside the bag, Vent gripped his lucky medallion and silently prayed as more and more of the terrible roaring voices rang out beneath him. Soon, a jubilant crowd of terrible Toxies had gathered as the dark gathered.

"We've got one! We've got one!" they sang together, dancing in the moonshadows. Toxies are very tiny Moxies and not only are their voices far too loud, all their gestures are extreme. They fling their arms wildly about, twitching their faces and wriggling their eyebrows as they bellow like titans.

Vent felt a sudden jerk on the rope that held the net up in the tree and then he was falling. *Thump!* Both of them, particularly the troll, who had fallen head first, were stunned. The troll kicked and bucked and hissed in rage, but the Toxies, who are also the most mischievous and spiteful of all Moxies, just laughed. Quickly, bellowing with glee, they cut him loose from the netting, and when the troll leapt out fiercely at them, hoping to break free, Vent remained where he was, silently trembling, unable to see his new captors. Only able to hear those huge and ferocious voices. Surely he must have been captured by wickees or even worse, werewolves.

For the rest of the night, the Toxies played a little game with the troll. First they formed a ring around him except they left an opening in their ranks, a space big enough for the troll to run through and escape. But anytime he got close to the opening and appeared to be ready to dart off into the forest, they would throw a sausage behind him. Then the troll would be torn — whether to escape or go for the sausage. And always this troll went for the sausage. Gulp! Gulp! Without even chewing the big greasy stinking questionable lumps of meat the troll stuffed himself while the Toxies watched and mocked. This went on till the troll was truly bloated and the Toxies were out of sausages.

"We tode you. No using the gates."

"We tode you," another of them screamed.

In answer the troll only whined in his high voice and stood pathetically still before them. Hoping to make him move, the Toxies now left a very wide opening in their ranks, but the Troll was waiting, hungry for more of the sausages. Or an attack. When he saw that they were neither going to attack him nor throw him more sausages he went wide-eyed and before them all he vomitted up all those greasy stinking sausages.

"Ooooooooooo" the sound of Toxie disgust reverberated through the night. The Toxies backed away, and in that moment the troll, snake-like, slithered away over the edge of the plateau and quickly disappeared into the waiting jungle.

Some of the Toxies wanted to chase after him, but just then one tiny Toxie noticed something shivering.

"Look — the bag! There's something else in the bag," she shrieked in a gale-force voice.

Quickly the little Toxie cut the rope that closed the mouth of Vent's bag and peered in.

"A little troll too!" she bellowed. "The big troll had a little troll in a bag on its back!"

"I'm not a troll," Vent protested. But he was still a little green from having been so dizzy and he certainly stank like a troll, having spent the night face down on a troll's back.

"It's a little troll!" the Toxie persisted.

"I'm not a troll," Vent repeated, trying to hide away deep in the bottom of the bag, but it was as though they didn't hear him.

"What are we gonna do with the little troll?"

"I'm not a troll."

"Detoxify the troll!" one of them shouted.

"Yes. Yes." There was a great cheer. "Detoxify the little troll!"

"No, no. I'm not a troll!"

"Come on, get the brushes and clamps. Get the soap. Let's —"

Just then there was an incredible shout from the Watcher's Rock where one of the Toxies was keeping look-out. "Quick!" was all he uttered and then, like a shadow into the last of the night, he was gone. Instantly forgetting whatever it was that trembled in the little bag, the other Toxies followed suit. They were there. There was a warning and like that they were gone. Like ink into ink, they were gone.

Inside the bag, all was silence. Suddenly the night was empty. No troll. No Toxies, just the chirping of a cricket, and . . . what was that soft rustling sound? Was it the wind?

21

Day of the Endless Night

By now Ogo had realized the terrible truth. Those dragons were no Moxie trick. They were true giant dragons. And this wasn't Co-Zee. Somehow he had come the wrong way. This was the great and ancient Wasteland of El-Oom. How that word chilled Ogo's blood. El-Oom. Where no magic works. Where there is no turning back. Where there is only one way out, and all hell in between. And he — with a child — in here. Here, where a child was a blasphemy, an object of hatred and envy. Trembling, he realized that he could no longer travel openly with Illia. He must wait till she slept, when he could hide her in his breastplate. For if any of the depraved denizens of this awful place saw her...

All that morning Ogo played with Illia in the meadow on the other side of Vharn where none might see them. His manner with her was merry indeed, but inside he was very worried. For hours they played her favourite games. They combed the doll's hair. They changed the doll's dress. They took the doll on trips. Horsee! Round and round they rode. They fed the doll and the doll flew. Then after lunch they read strange tales to the doll, and sang her songs. Finally Illia began to rock her doll, for the doll was very tired. And even as Illia rocked the doll, Ogo rocked Illia. After a very long time, the doll was fast asleep in Illia's arms and Illia was fast asleep in Ogo's arms.

The Blue Avenue had vanished but Ogo knew in which direction Orriador lay — to the east where the sun rose. He tucked Illia gently into his breast-plate with her beloved doll and he began to run.

Soon Ogo saw smoke on the horizon and there was a stench that could mean only one thing. They were approaching the Burning Place — the fabled Great Dump of antiquity. The cursed waste place of the ancient Moxie kings, right in the centre of El-Oom. Long ago there had been a terrible battle here and the gods had cursed the place, stripping it of all magic. Since then, whenever kings or queens had wished to rid themselves of magical devices such as lamps, horns, rings, cloaks, flutes and timbales, they had caused them to be dropped here, where they would lose their power.

Now all about him Ogo spied broken shards, shattered metals, half-sunken faces of stone that peered from piles of refuse and carnage. Bones, tools, tusks and tongs and everywhere burning dust and ashes.

116

Ogo ran as he had never run before. With a long-legged lope he wove his way among the piles, over the heaps, down in the valleys until finally he came to a swirling, steaming river. And here between a fire and a flood, he stopped, no way forward, no way back. The river, black and agonized, human voices, high Moxie voices rising from its mists, forbade entry. Ogo could feel its terrible heat as he drew close, and the water was wide — wider than any man could jump across. But Ogo was desperate and resourceful. He took that old jousting pole turned diaper pole and he ran towards the river full-tilt. Inches from the edge, he tilted the tip in and with the ease of a trained pole vaulter sailed safely over to the opposite bank.

All about him in the oozing soil, voices wailed. Old voices and young voices, human and Moxie voices, lost, fixed here, in this haunting place, trapped under the curse. And the further Ogo went, ankle-deep in mud, the more haunted and despairing the voices grew. "Justice! Justice!" they wailed. But Ogo had learned well the lesson of the Forest of Pleaders, and he continued on his way.

Suddenly a fearsome wickee darted in front of Ogo. At first Ogo was taken aback, and even in her sleep, Illia felt the jolt of his heart when he spied that demonic wickee face — bright red and horned! The wickee flashed a quick, terrible grimace and then was gone, but soon another one darted by. It too flashed a horrible look of torture, and then it too was gone, only to be replaced by yet another and another. Now Ogo began to spy wickees all around him, peering over rocks, hiding behind heaps of

117

trash, dashing from gush of smoke to gush of smoke. A wickee in the outside world is a most terrifying and powerful opponent, for wickees are well trained in the dark arts and enjoy nothing more than torturing any poor soul they can kidnap. But these wickees were just dancing around Ogo, trying to scare him with their pitiful horned faces. Why did they not attack?

The more wickees he saw, the more the terror in Ogo subsided. If this was the Wasteland — and it was the Wasteland — then these wickees could have no magical power over him and he knew it. And a Wickee without its dark magic is but a little weasely thing, all horn and scrawn, a little scarecrow of bones with a trident.

The wickees were getting desperate. This was the first knight to come through in a thousand years. A thousand years of eternity they had been exiled here, and now one bulging breasted knight came by and not a quiver of terror. Ogo only laughed.

"There's no magic here!" he sang. "No magic here!" And soon he began to see black-cowled wizards among the wickees, their hexagrams all useless, their wands but sticks. "No magic here! No magic here!" Ogo sang as he ran toward the east away from the setting sun.

And of course the farther he ran the darker it got. But even when the sun went down Ogo ran on, guided by the light of distant volcanoes. And then when this faded he found his way by starlight and by the eerie light of burning trash heaps. And then, starless, he proceeded by firelight alone, and then by no light at all, by...

118

Suddenly Ogo found himself in the most complete darkness he had ever known, for he had now come into that part of the Wasteland known as the Day of Endless Night. A place where no light had shone for a thousand years. He held his own hand up before his eyes but could not see it. Desperately he looked back the way he had come, hoping to find where that last source of light had gone out, but there was nothing in any direction. Just darkness.

But it was not an empty darkness. In fact, it was a densely populated darkness — a darkness full of shuffling spirits, trapped souls, unbottled genies, disappeared men and blind wickees, all of whom now began to wail and moan. Ogo felt his mind going and for a moment his terror was nearly out of control. But then Ogo remembered, once before, deep in the darkest cavern of his mountain home, he had felt the presence of a spirit. That night he had learned that the only power spirits had over the living was fear itself. And he knew something else about spirits. Ogo took out Illia's toy trumpet, an instrument he knew how to play, and as he walked he began to blow long, mournful notes, long blue tones of human music. The spirits were deeply moved and Ogo could feel them responding from their dark places. This was a darkness of the spirit. There was no magic in this place, and no light. But there *was* music.

Ogo played for many hours on the deep-toned horn as he walked and as the spirits wept. And then, when it seemed his song had touched the very bottom of sorrow, Ogo did what he loved to do best:

he began to make the music dance, undulating the notes, varying them in intervals of something like joy, something like celebration.

Soon Ogo was trumpeting to the heights in soaring bell-like tones of clarity. And something changed then, forever, in the Wasteland. For the spirits began to dance and that is when it is said the wickees were redeemed. For that is when all that magic energy the wickees had once used for evil was transferred into music and they took up all the cast-down trumpets, timbales and guitars that were there and began to learn to play them. But that is another story.

By now Ogo was tired. He had been running, weeping, laughing, carrying, herb-picking, doll-playing and horn-blowing for twenty-four solid hours and he was beginning to want to sleep.

Unfortunately he was also lost in the most impenetrable darkness. Darker than the deepest cave underground. But Ogo knew an ancient divining method from his grandmother that saved him. He still had the piece of lodestone in his pouch that his great-grandmother had given him. He took out his sword, which had no magic now — but this, they said, was science — and he rubbed the lodestone on it, magnetizing it. Then, balancing the sword on the point atop his helmet as he had been taught, he let it turn into the earth's ever-present magnetism. Even in the dark the sword responded, pointing north. Delicately Ogo felt with his hand to see the way it pointed. Knowing north, he knew which way was east and that was the way he proceeded.

From the darkest possible dark, as Ogo ran, the

sky became darkest deep black-blue, then heavy, heavy navy-blue, and then slowly while Illia slept and dreamed of giant dolls, the sky lightened. Ogo could feel the spirits falling away around him as the ground rose and fell beneath his feet. Up one hill, down another, up another high hill, down the other side, and the sky was dark purple now with shades of red and he could just barely see the sharp edges of the Heights of Gh'iz in silhouette, and still Ogo climbed and descended hills, growing ever more weary as he walked.

Just as the sky truly lightened and the deep day-blue of dawn started to show through the highest, most distant mountain clefts, Ogo felt Illia stir. Almost at the same moment, not too far off in a cave beside the bridge at Abognath, the Laughing Giant also awoke. And he was hungry. Very hungry.

22

Vent and the Dragons

Many centuries ago the dragons had come to live in the Wasteland, for few men ventured there, and they need not fear magic where there was no magic. But now that a man had been among them, terror too was among them, so they had flown fast away from Vharn all the previous day and well into the night from peak to peak all around the Wasteland, seeking safety.

Finally they had come to the highest peak of all — Gh'iz, right on the borders of El-Oom, Orriador and Awdor, and thinking that it might be safe here they began to land now, unaware of the Toxies who fled from them, and of the trembling figure who was just now peering out of the mouth of a sack.

Vent knew it would be best to stay as still as possible, but immediately upon seeing the dragons he began to shake. In fact, he shook so much his armour began to rattle. Hearing this, the gigantic she-dragon looked up startled. Vent felt his bowels rumbling and his hair rising as she waddled over toward him. There was only one chance now . . . Vent tore up out of the bag and began to run. This would have been very foolish if these had been man-eating dragons, for they could easily have caught him. But these were the dragons of El-Oom, who had never seen a man. As one, with great shrieks, their wings fluttered up and they ran from him, flying away like a flock of startled sparrows. Even as he himself was running, Vent watched this mighty retreat with amazement. His terror was deep, but his shame was working now too. And his shame was deepee.

Meekly, hoping to retrieve some dignity, Vent stopped his flight, reached for his bow and notched an arrow. Most of the dragons were out of arrow's reach by now, but that giant dragon was right over head and there was something tangled in its claws, weighing it down. Vent took aim.

Before he could loose the arrow, whatever it was the giant dragon had been carrying fell from the sky and beaned Vent right on the top of his head. Stunned, he picked himself up and tried to focus his eyes on the object. But even before he could see it properly Vent knew what it was, for there was a wonderful uplifting scent to it. A scent he knew only too well: garlic! And surely no other garlic could be so huge, so aromatic. This was the Great Garlic of Antibes!

Carefully, one eye to the skies lest the dragons return, Vent wrapped the garlic in the cloth it had

fallen in, slung it over his back and, scuffling from rock to rock, made his way down the far side of the mountain.

Soon he was walking in a land of profuse vegetation. Everywhere there were flowers, berries, pods, leaves, buds and melons, ancient barrows and vines, butterflies and petals, pelicans and peonies, roses by the billion and apples as large as your head.

Before long he found a blue road that ran east. And when he began to see windmills and waterwheels, Vent knew where he was. Miraculously, Vent was in Orriador!

Fub had travelled the fastest and gone the farthest with the least amount of trouble. In record time he had reached the estuary of Arn where the air was hot and humid. Now a signpost pointed away from the road Fub had been travelling, toward a narrow pathway that led into a forest. Cheerfully, but a little hot inside his heavy armour, Fub rode his poor tired horse into the forest. Soon the ground was softer and softer underfoot and the trees overhead darker and greener. There seemed to be little rivulets of water running everywhere and the path had become a path no longer but a muddy little creek. Indeed, it became so muddy the horse could go no further, no matter how hard Fub spurred and whipped it. Cursing, he dismounted his steed. "Lazy beast!" he shouted, landing ankle deep in the mud. Above him tree frogs chirped and the first of the fireflies flew by. Despite the increasing darkness it was still very hot and very wet. But Fub was not

125

deterred. He left the poor horse standing where it was, deep in the mud, and proceeded on foot, his metal boots squelching in the swampy earth. About his head as he trod deeper into the dense jungle, a halo of bugs began to whir. "Buzz! Buzz!" said Fub, swatting at them with his chainsword. Fub didn't know it, but he would arrive in Awdor very soon.

By bird, Moxie or magic, news travels quickly in Orriador, and so it soon came to Queen Blue's attention that a man who carried a snuggly was fast approaching Orriador along the road from Co-Zee. Only a mother could know the joy that moved in her to hear this news, for she assumed that this was the knight the King had sent to deliver Illia. Immediately she wanted to find the quickest horse in the nation and gallop to her daughter. But she was a queen and to some degree felt compelled to honour the rules of decorum which had been observed in Orriador since time immemorial. Besides, there was still much to do for the birthday celebrations. There were presents to be finished, tapestries to be woven, pastry chefs to observe and secret magic ingredients to be added to certain dishes. So Queen Blue did the responsible thing, something which, as a very young queen, she was not as yet well known for doing.

She waited. And as she waited she wove. And the more she waited, the more she wove, her hands moving magically fast, so that the images seemed to take shape in seconds before people's eyes. And the faster she wove the more she ran out of thread. And the more she ran out of thread the sooner she had an excuse to climb the 777 steps of the palace minaret to the room where she kept her spinning wheel so that she might get some more. Once there, with great impatience and longing in her heart, she would stare toward Co-Zee, hoping to catch just the smallest glimpse of her child.

But Vent was still too far away to be seen. Already, though, he had company. Already the Orriadorians had begun to walk along beside him, cheering, singing and dancing.

Vent, the griffin master, sure that all this cheering was rightfully for him, walked ever more proudly.

Still Queen Blue waited patiently in her palace, doing the Queenly thing. Not running out there. Not galloping out there to sweep her daughter into her arms. Impatiently she finished another tapestry and again she climbed the 777 steps to the top of the minaret. And this time there he was, within sight. A handsome young man, and there — that must be her beautiful daughter, in the snuggly on his back. Wouldn't you know it, sleeping right through her return.

Heart pumping with motherly joy, Queen Blue dashed down the stairs and almost high-tailed it out the palace doors to meet her daughter, but just in time she stopped, and with a steely calm forced herself to wait on the throne, weaving with her sister, Princess Berry-a-Gong, at her side. By now the acclaim of the crowds was so loud, so overwhelming that it was hard to hear anything else. Faster and faster Queen Blue's hands wove and waited.

Finally, just as Queen Blue's magical hands finished off still another tapestry, the palace doors

swung open and in stepped a rather slender looking fellow. Instantly from the back of the court,
looking over the heads of Moxies, Vent saw a pair
of eyes that stopped him in his tracks. No. Not
Queen Blue's green eyes. It was the darker, harder
eyes of Princess Berry-a-Gong that Vent looked
into, and a great thrill went through him. His hair
went up, he gulped and his life was changed
forever.

Quickly Vent strode through the wildly cheering
crowd to kneel at last before the throne and the
beautiful tapestries. Queen Blue stared eagerly,
incredibly patient as he continued to kneel.

"Yes, Yes. My child," she urged him.

"Huh?"

Vent stood back up as Queen Blue came down
from the throne.

"Show me. Show me."

Gloriously Vent unslung the burden from his
back, folded back the layers of the cloth and before
Queen Blue's eager gaze revealed the cute little
face of . . . a garlic!

"Waaaaah!" Queen Blue was so shocked, so startled she actually leapt back and shrieked.

"What is this?" Berry-a-Gong too had come
down from the dais and now stood imperially, glow-
ering at Vent, her eyes as dark as a hopeless night.
Vent stared back, swallowing and gulping. Not
understanding.

"My daughter. My daughter. Where is she, you
fool?" Queen Blue demanded fiercely. The Moxies
were not happy either. Their features were changing. They were looking very angry.

Finally Vent figured it out.

"Your Majesty," he said, trembling, "I fear there is a misunderstanding here." He paused, afraid.

"Tell her, knave, quickly," Berry-a-Gong commanded, and she actually pushed Vent with her foot.

"Ma'am." Vent returned Berry-a-Gong's stare with a look of defiance. "I am not the knight you think I am. I am Vent Pomandler."

"You were not sent to bring my daughter?"

"No, Your Majesty, I've just been through the Wasteland and I believe I have brought what must be a 'surprise' gift from the King."

"Ohhh. You mean some other knight —"

"A fellow named Ogo, Your Majesty."

"Who is yet to come!"

"He was sent out along the Blue Avenue, taking the long safe way around."

"I confess I have been a little worried," the Queen confided. "I have had an uneasy feeling."

"I believe she is in good hands, Your Majesty," Vent offered. "A very kind fellow and a highly skilled warrior."

Queen Blue looked very relieved but even more impatient.

"And what is this that you have brought, Vent?" she asked.

Vent gave a most splendid bow in the manner he had so excelled at in his school.

"As you can see — or should I say smell, Ma'am . . ."

Queen Blue inhaled deeply over the large bulb that Vent held before her.

129

"Why, it is the fabulous *Garlic of Antibes!*" she announced. There were murmurs of disbelief among the Moxies. Not in a thousand years!

"Please forgive me," Queen Blue spoke softly. "I apologize for calling you a fool when it is obvious you have achieved a very brave and difficult thing. I am sorry to have insulted you. Please understand that I am a mother and I am concerned."

"And how came he by this garlic?" Berry-a-Gong asked suspiciously.

"Most curious, Your Majesty." Vent turned to look straight into Berry-a-Gong's face. "I had the strangest luck. You see, in truth I must tell you that I was probably way off course in my journey through that terrible place, for I had been assailed by griffins and pterodactyls."

"You fought griffins?" Berry-a-Gong asked, still looking very suspicious.

"Why, yes," said Vent, for he still truly believed he had been through El-Oom.

"How brave," Queen Blue muttered, but she was hardly listening to him. She was thinking about her daughter and longing to see her.

"Yes, Your Majesty." Vent spoke to Queen Blue but it was still Berry-a-Gong he was staring at. "And I had a near-death experience with a troll and a searing squad of killer dragons. And I saw that one of them carried something. So I picked up my bow, I aimed it, and soon this garlic came tumbling down by I know not what great magic" — here Vent bowed again — "you must surely possess."

Queen Blue had turned toward Co-Zee whence

she knew her daughter would be coming.

"Princess Berry-a-Gong," she ordered. "I can stand it no longer. Please take a small greeting party and ride out to Co-Zee and meet this fellow who is bringing Illia and let us have her here with no more delay."

Berry-a-Gong snapped her fingers at several of her retinue and at once they gathered around her. Proudly she saluted the Queen and turned to leave.

"You'd better take this." Queen Blue held up her sceptre with the Orriadorian royal insignia on it. "Or the fellow might think you some kind of warrior and turn and flee from you."

Queen Blue laughed as she said this but she meant it, for in that moment Berry-a-Gong looked every inch the great and ferocious queen she would one day become. Berry-a-Gong plucked the sceptre from the air as Queen Blue tossed it to her and then she was gone. With her dark hair trailing behind her Berry-a-Gong darted from the palace and was soon astride her horse.

Off she and her retinue galloped and behind them went a huge motley mass of Orriadorians. Soon she would see Ogo and Illia, but she would be too late to change the course of events. For Ogo and Illia had already reached the gateway to Abognath, and their fate was upon them.

23

The
Laughing Giant

For the second day in a row Ogo played patiently with Illia, waiting for her to go to sleep in a treacherous and forsaken land. Not till that hour finally came, when her gurgling stopped and her breathing calmed, did he tuck her safely inside his armour and walk the last few steps before the gateway to Abognath.

It was the stench that first alerted him. A terrible coldness suddenly gripped his belly and an ancient animal fear arose in him. Something more terrible than dragons, something more wicked than wickees lived here. He had a great desire to run but when Ogo turned to retreat a heavy metal portcullis fell into place over the archway, blocking all exit. Quickly Ogo's eyes scanned the way ahead. He was at the bottom of a deep canyon whose walls widened gradually from the archway until they opened onto a plateau and there, at its far edge, was the longed-for bridge over the abyss. Half-buried beside it were the remains of a gigantic fallen statue whose one finger seemed to point ominously right at Ogo. Looking up, the canyon walls were unscalable, inhospitable and forbidding. What Ogo could not see because it had been cleverly disguised and covered with black ivy was the wide, dark mouth of a cave in the cliff side.

Like most denizens of the Wasteland, the Laughing Giant never seemed to get enough to eat. You couldn't tell this to look at him though, for he was quite round about the middle. But then he had a very narrow head for his size. And two-thirds of that was his great big jester's hat. Yes, the Giant had an under-sized head and he didn't like it. What he did like was laughing and eating. In fact he had two mottoes in life. One was "To laugh is human but to laugh at others is divine." The other was "If it walks, eat it."

He was always nabbing lazy warthogs, slow slugs, giant worms, dangling them up over his gaping, laughing mouth and then dropping them in. Food prep time was minimal. To him BASH! was cooking. WHACK! was a recipe. Anything living tasted good to him. But lately he had eaten only grubs and pigeons, wild hyenas and one old wickee who had wandered away from home. He sucked on the old bones now and giggled as he waited.

Sooner or later they all headed for the bridge. He knew that. It was the only way out. A magnet to wickees. Sooner or later, they all tried to sneak by.

133

Sometimes when this happened, he would stand and face the bridge and pretend he didn't see them coming up behind him. Other times he would just go into his cave, stick the back of his head out through a hole in the ivy so that you couldn't tell his greasy black hair from the ivy, and just sit and watch and wait. This was exactly how the Giant caught Ogo. Rubbing his hands together and drooling with anticipation, he saw Ogo dart from rock to rock until Ogo stood close to the mouth of his cave only a little way from the bridge.

Suddenly the Giant burst through the ivy, and facing Ogo head on with a rageful, earth-shaking stomp shouted "AHA!" in a voice of pure thunder that echoed off the cliff-side and down into the canyon over and over. "Aha . . . Aha . . . Aha . . ."

"What is this I see?" the Giant shouted far too loudly and then oddly began to giggle. "Is this a tin of wild bums that has learned how to walk? Is this one of those terrible creatures called a mite? I mean KNIGHT . . . knight . . . knight. I always get it wrong, ha-ha." Slapping his thigh and guffawing now, the Giant reached into the ragged robe he wore, removed a log-sized cigar and stuck it in his mouth. Ogo's heart beat louder and faster than he'd ever thought possible, as the terrible Giant thunderously and deliberately began to stomp toward him.

All his life Ogo had longed for this moment, but none of his dreams had been like this — caught unaware, frightened, with a baby to protect. With the first rush of terror he remembered his long-time plan — to make a sudden thrust upward with the sword tip and sever the Giant's tendon in the knee.

134

With light-speed calculation Ogo assessed this now. *Stomp! Stomp!* That space beneath the knee cap — cloth covered it. But who knew if there was armour under that? *Stomp! Stomp!* If he had only himself to worry about, Ogo would have fought whatever the odds. But he had so much more than his own life to lose now. Not only death but ignominy awaited him if the King's daughter were to die in his care. No, there was another tactic — one far less glorious but far more likely to succeed. Look at that Giant waddle. Swaying as he came. *Stomp! Stomp!* Borne down by his own sloth-like weight. All fat and pudge. Ogo would let him get as close as he dared and then he would dart through the astonished titan's legs at hyper-speed — just a blur and a look of upside-down rage as the Giant peeked between his own knees.

Humped and sinister, drooling a little stream of gibber from his agitated mouth, the Giant grinned intensely at Ogo as he approached across the titanic canyon floor. "Hey, canned man! You look ridiculous!"

Ogo held his shield before him and waited silent-ly. Yes, there was a wide space between the Giant's legs when he walked. And the Giant was slow. Just three waddling steps more and Ogo would make his dash. Even this was very risky but Ogo had faith in his own speed. *Stomp!* Just two more steps. Ogo tensed for the take-off. *Stomp!* One more step. As the Giant bent down to lunge at him Ogo darted. But he had made a terrible miscalculation. For this Giant was fast. Much faster than anyone thought and he loved to catch men in just this manner, by pretending he was slow. Dropping down on both knees so that he blocked the way forward he grabbed at Ogo with a shout of "Haaaa! I've got you!"

But he didn't quite have Ogo yet, for Ogo too had been very fast and he had stopped his flight just in time. Now, though, he was dangerously close to the Giant. Desperately, looking over his shoulder he saw the canyon wall behind him. Trapped! No way back and no way forward. And most terrifying of all, Illia was stirring.

The Giant stared down hypnotically upon Ogo, the remnants of a deep and tattered intelligence in his oversized face. Waves of glutinous flesh quivered and rippled across his slab-like cheeks. His mammoth lips trembled and he said, "I don't recall sending out for a snack." At this the Giant began to shriek with laughter, emitting such a terrible stink of rot and decay into the air that Ogo felt like throwing up, but he just stood there, stock still waiting for an opportunity to run.

"I see you've come in a nice metal container," the Giant continued. "What I call a squeeze pack." With this the Giant's hands moved so fast they were just a blur and in a moment he had grabbed Ogo. Terrified, Ogo managed to escape by letting go of his shield but now he was pressed right against the canyon wall.

"O look — a little serving platter." The Giant smirked and with one brutish gesture hurled the shield far away so that it spun and fell with a clatter into the abyss. "But I like to eat right from the can." The Giant continued to giggle insanely,

136

delighted at his own wit, but there was increasing rage in his mirth and his hypnotic eyes gazed ever more intently into Ogo's recoiling soul.

"Yes, yes, it comes in its own little cooking kit, doesn't it? Boil it. Bake it. Or eat it raw. Personally I like mine smoked." The Giant inhaled deeply on his reeking cigar and blew a great black gust at Ogo that nearly sent him keeling over with its gale-like force.

Now the Giant made another quick grab. Ogo side-stepped but it would not be long before the Giant had him. Ogo struggled to clear his mind of the smoke and the stench. To run now was impossible. But what about his other plan? The Giant's knees were temptingly close. One quick thrust up under the knee cap and this titan would topple.

"And do you come with your own cutlery?" the Giant mocked, a great stream of saliva dripping down from his gruesome mouth and hissing on the stone. His knee was as close as it would ever be for the Laughing Giant was moving in for the kill now, his eyes huge and glistening with excitement.

"Do you know my favourite vegetable?" he asked, in a trembling voice. Ogo said nothing. Suddenly the Giant smashed his fist upon the ground and shouted, "SQUASH!" But there was no laugh this time, just a wide, open reeking mouth licking its mammoth lips.

Lightning-quick, as the Giant raised his fist again, Ogo reached to unsheath his sword and he might right then have defeated the Laughing Giant by force of arms but at that very moment Illia woke up, terrified at the noise, and began to wail away inside his armour.

137

"Waaaaaa!"

Back and forth the Giant jerked his head double-take, his huge fist pausing mid-air over Ogo and Illia. "What was that I heard?" he asked, dismayed, and his shoulders shook so much with mirth the bells on his jester's cap began to tinkle. "Surely the canned man didn't let out a c-cry. A mewly little gurgle of terror!"

"Waaaaaaaa!" Again Illia cried out inside Ogo's armour, and her voice was loud. Very loud.

At this the Giant absolutely screamed with laughter.

Ogo's hand still hovered over his sword hilt but he saw that each time the Giant laughed he tilted his head way back. So Ogo did something very smart — he stuck his thumb in his mouth, wiped his eyes, clanged his knees together and began to mime the cries of Illia as though it were he and not she who was crying.

"O honour!" the Laughing Giant gasped and began to pound on his knee. "O great kings, hide your heads in shame. Never have I heard such a shameless little whine from a grown man. You are the most cowardly of all KNIGHTS!" At the word KNIGHTS the Giant pounded his house-sized fist so fiercely the very bedrock seemed to shake beneath Ogo. But he was just playing with Ogo, trying to make him cry out again. "Who dares not even FIGHT!" Again at the word FIGHT the Giant's great fist pounded the earth so powerfully Ogo fell over, causing the terrified Illia to cry even louder.

"Your valour of the MOUSE!" The Giant slammed his fist down and giggled again, enjoying the terror.

138

"And your sword that is the . . . the . . . laughing stock of swords." The Giant was laughing so hard now there were tears rolling down his cheeks, but Ogo could hear the laughter beginning to turn into insane rage. Any moment, he knew, the laughter might end and he and Illia would be doomed. He had to keep the Giant laughing. He *had* to. Swallowing his pride, breaking the last of his three oaths, Ogo fell to the ground and began to crawl in a most pathetic manner, wriggling like a worm while Illia wailed away inside.

This caused the Giant to fill up with a laugh that was so big at first he couldn't get it out. So he just leaned way back and yammered, pointing at Ogo and gasping for air, his shoulders shaking and his bells jingling.

Finally the over-sized guffaw exploded from him and for just a moment the Giant's head tilted so far back he lost sight of Ogo. This was just what Ogo had been waiting for. He shot out from his place against the canyon wall, dove through the Giant's legs and began to race toward the bridge.

There were about a hundred yards to the bridge and Illia was yelling like mad. The Giant turned in a rage and dashed after Ogo surprisingly fast. With Giant long legs. Way faster, way longer than any-one would have thought possible, ten strides of Ogo's for only one of this Giant's, and Ogo is dash-ing, darting, zooming to the bridge. He has only three steps to go but the Giant is almost upon him. Two more steps. One, two, he is up on the bridge, and the Giant is right there at the edge, reaching for him. But Ogo is too far across now and the Giant

139

is too big for the bridge. Oh, he knows he could destroy it if he wanted to. He could send this baby-man trickster hurtling down to his death. But then there would be no bridge. And without a bridge, why would wickees come by? And oh, oh, it was too late now, for Ogo was on the other side.

Ogo couldn't resist. Turning back toward the Giant he lifted his visor and said, "Haw-Haw" in his most mocking voice.

This was more than the Giant could stand. He began to scream in a titanic echoing bellow. Awk! Awk! Awk! No words, just Awk! Awk! Awk! until like some kind of gargantuan baby he began to cry. Then, when he went to wipe his eyes, he managed to burn his own forehead with the fiercely glowing cigar. Ssssss! AWK! AWK!

Ogo didn't stop to gloat. He just kept on running into Orriador. By this time Illia was deeply upset and angry. Desperately Ogo took her out and tried to comfort her. As much as it had hurt him to allow the Giant to insult him like that, as much as he felt humiliated to have crawled before this Giant, it hurt even more to have Illia cry like that.

Ogo might have thought that his progress was going unnoticed. But someone had noticed. Someone had seen him arrive across the bridge from the Wasteland. She saw him take out Illia and she watched enraged now as he tried unsuccessfully to comfort her.

24

Berry-a-Gong's Mistake

That someone was Princess Berry-a-Gong. When she arrived at the crossroads where the road from Co-Zee meets the roads from Awdor and El-Oom she had taken out her eyeglass to survey the territory ahead. Seeing no one, she looked into El-Oom and there she saw Ogo, just as he was crawling and squirming before the Giant, and even from this distance she heard the faint echo of a cry — a cry that she knew only too well — Illia!

"Come!" she shouted, and waving to her followers galloped headlong toward the bridge and Abognath. But by the time she had mounted the crest of the last hill, Ogo was already past the Giant and had crossed the bridge safely. She saw him turn back and mock the Giant. And then she saw him take the screaming Illia out of his breastplate and attempt to calm her down. Seething with rage, and

141

jumping to a wrong conclusion, Berry-a-Gong charged full-tilt down the hill toward Ogo, her retinue close behind.

"Seize him!" she commanded. "Seize him and bring the child to me."

"But . . ."

"Silence! I am Princess Berry-a-Gong of Gileador," she shouted. "And by the power invested in me by Queen Blue I order you to surrender the child to me."

"But . . ."

"Surrender the child to me!"

Here, for the first time in her life, Berry-a-Gong held up a royal sceptre in the air before her in a very threatening manner. Ogo saw the royal insignia of Orriador on it and he stopped.

Illia, seeing Berry-a-Gong, whom she knew well and loved, ceased crying for a moment and reached for her with a most forlorn look on her face. Ferociously Berry-a-Gong swooped down off her horse, took little Illia gently in her arms and then, burning with rage, she said to Ogo, "You were distinctly ordered by your King to take no foolish risks with Princess Illia. And yet you have dared risk her very soul in El-Oom for the sake of a cheap little chance at glory."

"But —"

"Silence! I command you."

Ogo was silent. "You shall soon see, Sir Canned Man Turtle, what the rewards of this valour will be. Queen Blue does not suffer adventurers well."

Illia had just spent far too long a time trapped inside Ogo's armour, being yelled at and threatened

142

by a giant, and unfortunately she too blamed Ogo. From the welcome shelter of Berry-a-Gong's arms she glowered at him and said, "Puh!"

Poor Ogo didn't know what to do. Every time he tried to speak, Berry-a-Gong silenced him.

"Boo!" Berry-a-Gong signalled to one of her courtiers, and a kind of ghostly looking Moxie sergeant stepped forward with a smile. "Please accompany this . . . glory seeker to the barracks and see that he is detained there until I can deal with him myself."

"Yes, Your Majesty."

The ghostly Moxie walked up to Ogo and, taking him by the arm, said, "Hi. My name is BOO! And I have been chosen to accompany YOU! Please come with ME."

Reluctantly Ogo began to walk off with BOO! as Princess Berry-a-Gong lifted Illia high up onto her horse.

Despite himself, Ogo was relieved to hear Illia chortle and burble with delight, happy to hear her sounding happy again, but just before she rode off, Illia turned back to him and pointing her finger angrily shouted, "Nay!" Then Berry-a-Gong spurred her horse, and in a great cloud of dust the two of them were gone.

So there was Ogo — Ogo who knew deeply that he had done the right thing, the most difficult and bravest thing, the only thing, in fact, and he was to be led off in shame, disgraced, misunderstood and silenced.

*   *   *

"You, sir, are being asked to confine yourself here," the guard said, no expression in her voice, as she led Ogo down the stairs to a blue cellar. "We will not chain you as it is not our way in Orriador, but we ask that you stay in this room. You may stand, sleep or . . . crawl if you like. But please do not leave this room."

"But what is to become of me?" Ogo asked.

"You are to be sent back whence you came as soon as possible," the guard answered. And then she closed the door.

Ogo had broken all three of his vows: he had turned away from creatures who requested help (so what if they were evil djinns?); he had slept unknowingly among dragons (so what if all anyone could smell was garlic?); and worst of all he had crawled and cried before a giant (so what if it was the surest way of saving Illia's life?). Ogo had gone wrong, surely. But somehow in his heart he felt that he had followed the King's commands to the letter and he could not believe that he deserved this — to be restrained in a cell, to be misjudged and exiled without a chance to speak his peace. The injustice of it welled up in his throat. Then, when he heard the sound of distant trumpet blasts and cheering as Illia was returned to her mother's joyful arms, Ogo hung his head and cried.

25
Birthday!

It was a warm summery evening in Orriador and everybody had come from everywhere — not just Orriadorians, but birds, lizards, little trolls, Moxies and others. All the sky had that smell of woodfires as the palace chefs cooked a great Pasta of the People.

Throughout the evening, the palace filled up with the many Peoples of the Endless Day until there were creatures everywhere. On parapets, ledges, pinnacles, on outcroppings and ornaments. Perched on the shoulders of statues and peering over the edges of doors. Big and small, they filled up the great palace with their pasta and multitude and as many as could fit sat around the Great Blue Table.

All this Ogo missed as he wept down in his blue basement room. Had he been able to see Vent, his heart might have been pierced even more, for just then Vent, standing next to the wild Princess Berry-a-Gong, was receiving a great commendation from Queen Blue herself, thanking *him* for his heroic retrieval of the Garlic.

"O assembled hosts of Orriador," Queen Blue said when she had finished addressing Vent. "I welcome you all most gratefully to this banquet. As you may have heard, this occasion is doubly significant, for not only is it the first birthday of my daughter, Princess Illia, who shall be with us presently, but also we have harvested the Great Garlic of Antibes. And we shall be the first in many a long year to know the savour of a Great Pesto of the Tribes."

There was a huge cheer as the assembled creatures banged their cups and bowls and thimbles on the stone table in a cacaphony of tapping and ringing.

When this had subsided the radiant and smiling Queen Blue continued. "Those of us who have been charged to do so must now inhale this heavenly pasta. And then we shall see what we shall see."

And so did the great chomping and sipping begin. There was garlic bread, garlic butter, garlic spaghetti, and of course garlic pesto. Garlic, garlic, garlic and dew, dew, dew everywhere — in decanters, goblets, bottles, casks, flagons. To and fro, the palace porters walked, carrying trays, pitchers, platters full of garlic and dew.

Suddenly there was a great trill of flutes, a blast of bugles and . . . "All welcome Princess Illia!" Illia was carried in waving away as usual, and all rose as one and cheered.

From the comfort of her mother's arms, Illia looked all up and down the long table. She saw the many loving faces of her family and neighbours and

146

friends and great joy entered her heart. But something was missing.

There was an expectant pause. In the sudden quiet — a quiet when normally someone would show up with a birthday cake — Illia said "Ogo!"

"What was that?" Queen Blue asked.

"Ogo!" Illia shouted, looking all around.

Many of the Moxies thought this was some kind of cheer so they repeated after her, "Ogo!"

"He's the fellow — the commoner..." Vent advised Queen Blue. "The one who brought her."

Illia turned to her mother. She shrugged her shoulders in a way that she had learned from Oolus, a way that meant, "Hey, where is ..." And then she said again, "Ogo." And the walrus, the wolverines and the Moxies all shouted out "Ogo" quite loudly, as it was a nice word to shout anyway.

"Oh, the fellow who brought her." The Queen had been so busy she hadn't even thought of him. "Of course. Where is he?" Queen Blue turned to Berry-a-Gong, who was standing very close to Vent.

"Ma'am, I was hoping you wouldn't have to spoil your birthday celebrations by having to deal with this," Berry-a-Gong said apologetically. "There was a small problem with the fellow so I arranged for his, uh ..."

"Ogo!" Illia demanded haughtily.

Queen Blue heard something in Illia's voice that meant more to her than words.

"But whatever did he do? Why is he not here?"

"Well, Ma'am." Berry-a-Gong was hesitant to tell the whole upsetting truth to Queen Blue, so she told only part of the truth. "He broke his oath to the King."

147

"Oh. His oath to the King."

"Yes, Ma'am. I can give you the details later but I thought it would not be seemly to have him here at this moment." Already Queen Blue knew that something was not right.

"And has he absorbed the terrible importance of his mistake?" she asked.

"I believe so, Your Majesty. I am told he is weeping."

"I see, and has he . . . apologized?"

"Not actually, Ma'am."

"Well, what has he said for himself?"

"Well . . . nothing yet, Ma'am."

"You did not let the fellow speak?"

"I'm sorry, Ma'am. I did not wish to endanger Illia . . . any further." Berry-a-Gong was very upset and she looked to Vent for support.

Now the Queen asked most intently, "What do you mean 'any further'? What was this fellow's crime?"

"Ma'am. He did not go through Co-Zee as the King ordered him," Berry-a-Gong answered.

Queen Blue's eyes narrowed. "Which way *did* he go?"

"Ma'am, he went through . . ." Berry-a-Gong looked to Vent again.

". . . The Wasteland." Vent finished the statement for her.

There never had been such a hush. Not a peep, a *gawp!* or a *doing!* in the whole hall. Just Queen Blue wide-eyed, and Berry-a-Gong and Vent holding hands without even knowing it.

"Bring him to me," was all Queen Blue said.

"Yes, Ma'am." Berry-a-Gong sent Boo to retrieve Ogo.

148

It must be pointed out that Vent was not deliberately lying. Even now he still somehow believed that he too had crossed the Wasteland. But there was a very strange feeling in Vent's stomach when Ogo finally approached and knelt nervously before the Queen.

"Arise," she commanded, and Ogo, his head still bowed, stood up, a big blush rushing over him.

"Young man, you have been called here to answer unto me before these hosts."

Ogo said nothing. Perhaps his blush deepened. He felt Illia's spry eyes staring at him.

"What is your name?"

Now Ogo had one of those embarrassing moments that he thought he'd finished with when his voice had stopped changing. For when he went to say the O in Ogo, his voice somehow slipped from the deep manly register he had acquired and slid way up for a second into a falsetto with a kind of gulp on the way, so that he said "O-ooo-Go." Everybody even Illia laughed, but the Queen continued to stare at him severely.

"Ogo, I am told that you took my daughter through the Wasteland."

Ogo whispered, "Yes, Ma'am."

The Queen visibly hardened. Her eyes grew very piercing.

"Did the King not tell you to take her through Co-Zee?"

"Yes, Ma'am."

"Did he not tell you to keep unto the Blue Avenue all the way and to take no risks?"

"Yes, Ma'am. B-but —"

"But you decided to go through the Wasteland instead in search of glory. You —"

Here Ogo actually spoke up. He couldn't stand it any longer. In a quite loud voice he said, "It was a mistake, Ma'am."

"You're quite right it was a mistake!" Queen Blue shouted. She was so angry that Ogo lost his nerve again and became silent. Fortunately, just then the Queen noticed the big bulge in his breastplate. "But what is that?" she asked.

"Ma'am, this I designed specially for your daughter that she might draw comfort from my skin and be protected."

"Why would a man take such care and then risk all?" the Queen wondered to herself.

By now Vent had almost got that strange feeling in his belly worked out. Beside him Berry-a-Gong glowered at Ogo, clenching her fist.

"Go on," Queen Blue said.

"Ma'am," Ogo was trembling. He was almost as scared as when he'd faced the Giant. "Ma'am, I swear I did not deliberately go into the Wasteland. I went the way the signs pointed...but when I emerged I came out in a strange forest where trapped spirits pleaded."

"The Wasteland," Berry-a-Gong affirmed, staring fiercely at Ogo.

"I would not knowingly have risked your daughter's life, Ma'am."

Here, to his credit, Vent spoke up: "Ma'am, I think the signpost might have been changed."

"The signpost?"

"Yes, Ma'am," said Ogo, looking gratefully at

150

Vent. "I truly went the way the signposts pointed."

"Dangungs!" spoke Illia.

"Yes, I knew not that we were near dragons, Ma'am," Ogo confessed humbly. "I'm so sorry. You see I thought we were in Co-Zee."

"You were among dragons!" the Queen almost shouted, holding her hand over her heart.

"Yes, Ma'am, and that was how I lost the Great Garlic, you see —"

"Slow down!" the Queen commanded, still eyeing him severely. "I want you to take a deep breath and tell your story from the beginning."

And so, with the Queen's encouragement, Ogo humbly told his tale. He told of the Forest of Pleaders and his mother's oath. He told with full honesty of his sleeping with dragons and his journey through the Night of the Endless Day. When he got to the part about his encounter with the Laughing Giant, thousands of Moxie mouths hung wide open with amazement and Queen Blue turned almost white. As he continued the Queen held Illia tightly to her bosom, hardly breathing until Ogo had finished. Then there was silence. Complete silence.

Ogo hung his head in shame and waited. He wanted to apologize again but he didn't have to say more, for it was now quite clear to Good Queen Blue that this was an extraordinary fellow. She had seen clearly into his honest eyes as he spoke. And despite her fright, she had sensed the pain and shame of the injustice he was feeling.

"O all of Orriador and more!" she called out at last, suddenly smiling broadly. "Look ye upon this great fellow here who has done the bravest, most delicious

151

thing!" With that the Queen came forward, threw her arms around Ogo's neck and gave him a big, regal, queenly hug such as few men receive, even kissing him on the cheek so that another big geyser of blush blood went shooting through him.

"Wo!" was all Ogo said, as everyone cheered joyfully.

"But if the signs were changed," Berry-a-Gong asked, "and this fellow went into the Wasteland, which way did you go, Vent?" Berry-a-Gong looked deeply into Vent's eyes. He went very white, very quickly, and he said in a kind of gaspy whisper, "I *thought* it was the Wasteland, Ma'am."

"And how big were those griffins?" Berry-a-Gong asked, her eyes dark as hurricanes and full of sunsets in ancient lands that Vent would never see.

Vent made a motion with his hands that showed a length of —

"Puppies!" Princess Berry-a-Gong snorted with disgust. "You were in Co-Zee all along." Vent did not know it at the time, but those would be the last words this Princess would speak to him for many years. He said nothing at first. He just hung his head in shame, feeling like the unluckiest knave alive. Then another part of the story suddenly became clear to him.

"But Your Majesty," Vent asked, "if indeed the signs were changed — who then changed them?"

Before anyone could think on this there was a shout outside the palace and a desperate pounding on the door.

"Help! Help! Oh prithee let me in!" a strangely familiar voice was shouting.

152

26

Ogo's Choice

When the door was opened, the almost naked man who came jumping and swotting and swinging toward them looked familiar. And perhaps there was a swarm of fleas or flies going by just then, for everybody at first heard a strange *Zzzzzzz* sound as he entered.

"Why, it is Fub!" said Ogo. "He was sent out against the Might of Awdor."

Fub, lunging about spasmodically, bucking and jolting from the hips, twitched and twisted his way toward them as though being poked by tiny invisible pins.

"Aaaah!" Fub screamed, and the strange *Zzzzzzzz* sound followed him. "Shelter! Shelter! Please, a covering for my body. Please, I beseech thee." Mercifully, Queen Blue took down one of the large billowing Orriadorian flags and passed it gingerly

153

to Fub. "You may find shelter in this." So saying, she snapped her fingers and suddenly the strange buzzing stopped.

Fub pointed meekly to a place beneath the stone table and without even waiting for permission he ducked quickly under it and crouched there, still looking terrified. "You see, I was sent on a quest in which I encountered some supreme resistance."

"You were sent against the Mite of —"

"Awdor, Ma'am. Yes." Fub nervously cut in.

"Do not interrupt me again." Queen Blue spoke sharply, causing Fub to twitch like a frightened animal.

"No, Ma'am."

"So how come you in nothing but your underwear to my feast?" Queen Blue asked, severely.

"Well, Ma'am, you see, I did not realize when His Majesty sent me against the Mite of Awdor that he actually meant mite as in — you know, a tiny wee little parasitic insect. I thought he meant mite as in MIGHTY. And so I went out mighty, ready to meet the Might, to defeat the Might. Unfortunately in the middle of the night I met the Mite His Majesty actually meant — the terrible little zzoooooming, wild flying mite as in termite and I tried and I tried to smite that mite but to no avail."

The whole court including Queen Blue laughed out loud.

"O, you thought the Mite of Awdor meant the entire might of Awdor. Why, you poor ignorant man. This must be the work of Oolus." The gathered hosts laughed again and Fub appeared to blush.

154

But Fub had more to tell. "I was sore tried, Your Majesty. I swung and I swung. I tried to smite the mite but the more I smote the more it buzzed and dodged my mighty sword till soon I was tired. And then, cold as Pluto it somehow got in under my halberd and began shooting around in my armour, Ma'am, so I had to remove it piece by piece. Till I was left with only what you see me in now. But even then I was not yet defeated, for I am no normal m —"

Some say that Illia caused what happened next. For Fub, seeing that the Mite no longer pursued him, was slowly beginning to regain his confidence. This was not an easy thing for a man in his position to do. He was just breathing into it, puffing up his chest, when, some say, Illia saw again that arrogant man who had bashed her doll with Baaam the Lamb. With a little sideways twist of her head and a clap of her hands she made what some say was a magic sound. She went, "Zzzzzz."

Instantly that strange buzzing returned — only louder. Much louder. A sound like a thousand locusts at once. Instantly Fub was out from under that table, shrieking in a high voice, his hand helplessly trying to cover him as the Mite dove under his last remaining piece of clothing. Screaming, he ran at first in circles and then farther and farther afield, begging and pleading for mercy while everyone laughed helplessly. Queen Blue snapped her fingers again but it only seemed to make the buzzing louder. With nothing to aid him now, Fub headed for the door, and as his screams grew quieter in the distance so did the terrible buzzing.

155

"Poor fellow," the Queen said. "But he will wear it out soon, I'm sure. Someone apprehend him and run him down with mistletoe. Take him to my quarters until I can attend him."

"Poor fellow." Vent was not laughing.

"Imagine trying to fight a bug with a broadsword," Queen Blue sighed. "Perhaps he will learn now that not all problems can be solved by the sword."

"Yes. Yes," Vent and Ogo nodded to one another.

"And what of you two?" the Queen asked them as Illia continued clapping her hands and going "Zzzzzzz" and laughing. "Did your weapons aid you on your quests?"

"I never actually shot a single arrow, Your Majesty," Vent confessed under Berry-a-Gong's penetrating gaze.

"My mother told me my sword would be the envy of swords and yet it served me only as a spade to dig up the garlic," Ogo spoke mournfully. "Plus, I have broken all three of my oaths to the King."

"And yet," said Queen Blue, holding up her precious Illia so that all could see her, "you are victorious."

Somehow Ogo didn't quite feel victorious.

"You know, we have a saying here in the Lands of the Endless Day," Queen Blue continued, smiling at Ogo. " 'The greatest victory is not to have to fight.' And even though you feel you had to break your oaths and humiliate yourself, you did it in the service of human life and common sense — and that, Ogo, is no sin. In fact, it is a great virtue in you."

157

"I hope the King will agree with you."

"Oh, I assure you he will," the Queen replied with a very musical and enthralling laugh.

All this time Illia had been watching Ogo. She didn't fully understand what had happened in the Wasteland. All she knew was that she'd had a lot of fun with this fellow and had grown to love him very dearly for his gentle manner and wonderful songs. Standing up in her mother's arms, she reached out to Ogo and said, "Uh-uh!"

"Look, she wants to go to you." Queen Blue was delighted. "I think you've made a friend for life here, Ogo."

A little sob of joy moved in Ogo's breast. "My little dangung!" he said very gently as Queen Blue passed the little one to him. Instantly Illia snuggled into her favourite place against his chest.

"As you must know, Ogo," Queen Blue spoke so that all could hear, "today is Illia's very first birthday and we will soon be bringing out rather too many gifts for her, but you have shown such good sense and courage in your journey that I wish also to grant you a boon. Upon coming into our order of the Endless Day, all would-be knights are usually assigned a lifelong quest by their King or Queen. But you, Ogo, because you have shown such unusual courage and service, and because I believe in the right to choose — I will let you pick your own quest."

Everyone gasped.

"Uh . . . uh . . . Such an honour . . ." Ogo blushed and blanched and blushed again. "I'm stunned."

"What will it be?" Queen Blue persisted.

158

"Wow. Sheeze . . . This is — so difficult. Uh . . . You know . . . First I think — dragons. Slay those dragons . . . and then that awful giant laughter rings in my ears. And always that terrible galloping of the horse I —" Ogo was on the verge of making his decision when Illia actually spoke her first sentence.

"Ogo go go?" she asked.

"What?" Ogo was thrilled. "Did she say Ogo? Did she finally say my name?"

Queen Blue just smiled as though this had all happened a thousand times before and she knew exactly what was going to happen next.

"Ogo go go?" Illia asked again in a sad little voice.

"She did!" Ogo twirled her around joyfully in his arms, forgetting for a moment that she was a Princess and that he was in the presence of a Queen. "She *did* say my name. Oh my — My Majesty, now I *do* feel victorious. I have decided. I wish to be this baby's guardian knight! To keep her safe and attend to her happiness forever."

Ogo had hardly finished this statement before the big gasp of Moxie lungs and the great hoot of Moxie joy overwhelmed him.

When this joyous accolade had ceased Queen Blue took Ogo's own sword and with it she gave him the title that was to stay with him all his life, and long after into the history books. "Henceforth you shall be known," she said, touching his shoulders, "as Sir Ogo . . . of Babies." Now there was another even bigger hoot of joy from the assembled tribes.

159

"A cheer for Sir Ogo of Babies," shouted Berry-a-Gong, and they all answered her, "Sir Ogo of Babies! Sir Ogo of Babies!"

This was a most joyous and perfect moment in Orriador. Hardly had the shouting and cheering for Ogo died down when servants finally emerged holding the magnificent twelve-tiered birthday cake. There was another cheer from everyone there and then they began to sing the Orriadorian birthday song.

Oh, happy is your mother,
Who gave you birth.
You're a child of time
And a babe of the earth.
Happy earth day,
It's your birth day,
Happy green grass in dew,
Happy earth day,
It's your birthday,
Happy birthday to you.

Oh praise to your father,
He gave you such care.
Oh drink the sweet water
And breathe the sweet air.
It's your earth day,
Happy birthday,
Happy sunshine in blue.
Happy earth day,
It's your birthday,
Happy birthday to you.

160

From her very comfortable place in Ogo's arms, Illia took her mother's hand, leaned over the brightly dancing candle-flame on top of the great cake and, with one well-aimed breath, blew it out!

Epilogue

The next day, Ogo took Illia out for a walk and she began to point at something off in the distance and say her one sentence again. "Ogo go go!" she said. But this time it wasn't a question, it was a command. "Ogo. Go! Go!" Sensing the presence of magic, Sir Ogo walked in the direction she was pointing out over a field, across a meadow and up a hill, until finally in front of a huge grey boulder beside a golden stream she began to make one of her favourite animal sounds. It was the very first sound that Ogo had taught her from her magic book. A kind of high-pitched whinny — a sound quite like that of a horse. Ogo's heart thumped with an amazing thrill as something stepped out from behind the rock. It was *the* horse. The horse he'd seen that day on the mountain with Illia. The horse he'd always dreamed of. And neighing softly, it walked right up to him and nuzzled his face.

Acknowledgments

K*nights of the Endless Day* was first told as a bed-time story to my step-son Ananda in September 1984 on the occasion of the birth of his brother, Eli. It was published as a short story entitled *The Knight and the Baby*, in *Now* magazine in January 1986. During a writer-in-residence program at Mixed Company Theatre in 1989, I developed it into a short play. This play was then expanded during two workshops and a production at Young People's Theatre, where it ran in early 1992 under the title *Knights of the Endless Day*.

Throughout this long course of creation, input, interpretations, images and energy came from many people. I wish to acknowledge and thank the crew of YPT's production of *Knights of the Endless Day*: artistic director Maja Ardal, director Jennifer Stein, set and costume designer Shawn Kerwin, lighting designer Paul Mathiesen, composer Ted Dykstra, choreographer Alejandro Ronceria, fight director John Stead, stage manager Tony Ambrosi, and assistant stage managers Henry Bertrand and Laurie Hirst; and the cast: Lindsay Collings, Oliver Dennis, Melanie Doane, Kyra Harper, Jani Lauzon, Rick Roberts, Cliff Saunders, and Jim Warren, as well as workshop members Christina Nichol, Andy Massingham and Alison Sealy Smith.

Thanks also to Marsha Kirzner, Alice Klein, Ross MacDonald, Carol Bolt, Maja Ardal, Fiona McCall, Cynthia Good and David Kilgour. Special thanks to Allen Booth for his encouragement and many helpful suggestions. And to Ananda for letting the story be told.

I also wish to thank the Ontario Arts Council for its support during various stages of the creation of this tale, and many other projects.